ABOUT THE AUTHOR

M. L. Tompsett is an emerging contemporary romance author — and this is her eighth book published. She has been crafting worlds to escape to since she was a little girl. Years later, she continues to enjoy writing in imaginative, make-believe worlds filled with exciting characters, diverse locations, and various tropes as she ventures into the large, wide, and scary world of digital and print book publishing, including audio.

Married to her childhood sweetheart, they reside in Victoria, Australia, and have two extremely talented adult sons. M. L. Tompsett is thrilled to see something she has been creating become a reality as a published book.

When she's not typing away on her keyboard for the next page-turning novel while sipping tea and munching on licorice, she's busy working on digital files for one of her many talented clients' next book releases — or capturing random scenic photos around Australia.

Check M. L. Tompsett out on her website, blog, or social media.

www.mltompsett.com

facebook.com/M.L.TompsettAuthor

instagram.com/mltompsett.author

bookbub.com/profile/m-l-tompsett

ALSO BY M. L. TOMPSETT

CONTEMPORARY ROMANCE

SECOND CHANCE AT LOVE - series

Insta Bride

The Bodyguard's Convenient Marriage

Ghost of a Chance in Love

Secret Heiress

<u>**Paranormal Fantasy**</u>

Sex, Lies And Family Secrets - series

The Guy Next Door - Book one

Dark Surprises - Book two

You Never Know - Book three

It's You - Book four

What You Know - Book five

Other Vampire books

Her Vampire Fated Mate

Urban Fantasy

Shifter Romance

Kept in the Dark of Love and Lust

Kept in the Dark of Lies and Deceit - book two

Non-Fiction

My Travel Log
(Print Book Only)

Ghost of a Chance in Love

Contemporary romance with paranormal themes

M. L. Tompsett

SECOND CHANCE AT LOVE

Tompsett Publishing™

For my Family.
Love you guys.

Also

To all my readers who have given me the chance to continue to write a new genre.

Thank you

♡

This is for you.

♡

♡

To you, the reader

Please, have a medical check-up. This year
several people I had known have died or are
fighting for their lives, for reasons which could
have been avoided.
Have your moles and spots checked.
Have a mammogram.
Do your stool test.
Have yearly full blood work done.
If you cough or pass, blood, have it checked as
soon as possible.
If you just don't feel right and it continues more
than a few days — and it is out of the norm for
you — Don't leave it thinking it will go away.
Go to your doctor.
Life is far too short.

♡

BLURB

Love, mystery, secrets, and a ghost. Who can you trust?

One windswept Chicago autumn, teenager Laini Raiker's life changed forever. The mafia murdered her parents, and she's tossed into protective custody, starting life with nothing but a new name with a new family. Eighteen years later, Laini was blissfully married to the love of her life, Jaxton Travelli, until she woke up in the hospital staring down at her comatose body. How the hell did she get there? Did her now-missing husband abandon her? Refusing to believe the worst, Laini is determined to discover the truth. As she delves deeper, a web of lies emerges as long-lost enemies surface, threatening to destroy her family and everything she believes in. But time is running out. With the mafia closing in, how can Laini save her missing husband when she is a ghost? How is she to save herself before she becomes permanently spirit bound?

Love and loyalties are tested in this plot-twisting, romancing, mystery, action-packed, who-can-you-trust, page-turning book.

Ghost of a Chance in Love

Trust in yourself
Believe in your abilities
You can take the next step forward life throws
at you.
Your future is in your hands
Start your new chapter today.

— *M. L. Tompsett*

Oh, gypsy sticks.

You got to be kidding me.

Not at my age!

I have a teenage daughter, for goodness sake.

Maybe the result will be different if I close and then open my eyes.

Here goes...

My eyelids flutter shut — I count to five, then slowly open them, stare down and focus.

You've got to be kidding me.

No.

Oh, fudge knuckle — no.

My mind does not want to comprehend what I am staring at. Yet...I cannot believe it — the result is the same!

My breathing quickens as my heart thumps against my ribs. Darkness fills the edges of my vision as I become light-headed. My knees buckle from under me, and thankfully my butt lands on the closed toilet seat.

How did this happen? Of course, I know how it can happen, but how did it actually happen to me?

I keep reminding myself — *Breathe, Laini. Remember to breathe! Please don't let me pass out.*

I glance back towards my sister's bathroom vanity and again shut my eyes, hoping what I am witnessing is not real.

Surely it cannot be — my mind is playing tricks on me.

My breath races as I slowly open my eyes and blink, focusing on the two long plastic beacons of turmoil displaying the matching result on their little screen.

Come on, Laini, get your shit together, I chant.

I close my eyes to concentrate on calming my breathing. Then, after a few seconds or maybe minutes later, I slowly open my eyes, and the word stating *pregnant 3+* stares right at me.

No. No. Noooo.

My skin begins to tingle — the soft tingle feeling increases to the familiar buzz sensation my familiar spirit ghost causes every time she is near. At least I know my body is not causing that reaction as I glance to my side. Floating, there is Betsy, my spiritual guide and ghostly friend.

Using my mind to communicate with her, I demand, *'How could I be pregnant?'*

She glances at the pregnancy tests and smiles. *'Laini pet. It says it's positive. You're pregnant.'*

I would roll my eyes at the woman if I were not so stressed out. But all I can manage is a nod.

I first met Betsy, as a spirit ghost back in Chicago.

The couple who had given birth to me had purchased her house. It was only twenty months later, my parents were killed and the house burnt to the ground. I had been placed in protective custody. And as an adult I discovered the couple I went to live with were actually my biological parents.

'Betsy, what am I going to do?'

'You'll be fine, Laini pet. Congratulations.'

"Laini, time's up," my sister screams through the bathroom door, making me jump. "What's the result?" What's the result she demands? Well, it's a shock. That is the bloody result. Of all the things to happen at my age. Aren't I too old to be pregnant? "Come on, Laini. What does the test say?"

I gulp and stare at the door.

"Shit... Essy," I squeak. I glance back at the dreaded sticks. "How in the world can I be pregnant at my age?" I moan. My eyes begin to mist up. "I have a thirteen-year-old daughter. Surely I'm too old?"

I hear an unladylike snort come from behind the door. "Maybe don't have unprotected sex," Essy mumbles, then wobbles the door handle. "Open the bloody door," she says louder. "Give me a look at the stupid stick. Did you remember to use the second test as a backup?"

'Go. Your sister is here. Allow her to be there for you.'

I nod at Betsy. She then vanishes before my eyes leaving me alone. I stand, run my hands over my face, making sure no tears have escaped, and pick up both tests. Then, inhale a deep breath as I lift my chin and stand tall with my shoulders back, hoping to fool myself that I am stronger than I appear.

As my fingers reach for the door handle, I pause. *My life is about to change in a big way.*

I pull open the door, swinging it wide, and say, "Yeah. Yeah. Of course, I used both of them. They say the same thing." I glance towards Essy, then back to the pregnancy tests in my hand, and smile. "I'm pregnant!"

Chapter Two

ESSY

OMG. I knew it!

My sister is pregnant after all these years. Wow! I'm going to be an aunt again.

From all those years ago, when I first met Laini at her Chicago high school as an undercover student for the FBI — she would later become my adopted sister — only to discover years after that we were indeed blood-related and that our adoptive parents were our biological parents. Strange and mysterious how different events in one's life happen.

Joy fills me, and I begin to smile at my sister. "Wow. How do you feel about it?"

She smiles. Her eyes meet mine, and then she frowns. "I'm not sure. Don't get me wrong. But, am I ready?" Her eyes mist up.

Silly girl. I wrap my arms around her shoulders and give her a tight squeeze. "Yes, Laini, you are ready. You have been ready for a long time. Only this time, your husband can be by your side."

Laini married her long-time love several years ago, who is also the father of their thirteen-year-old daughter.

When Laini was seventeen, she found herself pregnant. However, before she could inform her boyfriend, he would be a father. He was sent away by his parents. It was later revealed that his parents refused to acknowledge Laini and quickly organized an arranged marriage for their only son. After all those years apart, Laini and Jaxton have a second chance at life and love.

"What am I going to tell Jax?"

"What you should have said to him fourteen years ago."

"Essy, don't be a bitch." Oooh. Touchy. I only wish I had known about her teenage pregnancy. I could have been there for her. Instead, our mother hid her away until after the baby was born. In all that time, Mother had made it look as if Laini was overseas backpacking through Europe, sending regular postcards.

"I was honest, Laini. It's time for the two of you to grab life and enjoy it. Now you have a new baby to enjoy."

"But."

"No, buts. Go make an appointment with your doctor and have the pregnancy confirmed." I wiggle my eyebrows and smile. "Then surprise your husband with the news."

Her worried frown turns into a smiling face of excitement. But then, it might be how Laini thinks of her husband. Several years ago, Laini and Jaxton surprised us with a dinner party. We thought it was to announce they were getting married. Instead, the dinner party was to celebrate their first wedding anniversary. Our parents were not impressed with another daughter getting hitched without them being there to witness the ceremony.

Even after all this time, Laini and Jaxton still act like two teenagers in love.

"Okay, Essy. I'll phone my doctor's clinic."

I turn and watch my fun-loving sister go to her handbag and remove her cell.

Right then, that's my hint to give her some privacy.

*W*ith my steaming cup of tea sitting between my hands and another hot brew waiting opposite me on my kitchen table, I wait patiently for Laini to walk into the kitchen.

Geez, how long does it take to make an appointment?

Laini's light footsteps sound from the hallway before her easy-going treads echo behind me.

I shift my laptop and paperwork to the side and concentrate on Laini as she sits opposite me.

She reaches for a chocolate cookie, specially imported from Australia — original chocolate TimTam's from the plate on the table. She dunks it in her cup and quickly sucks the yummy melting chocolate between her lips before eating it.

I shake my head at her antics. But unfortunately, my adorable sister never changed that habit. She still eats chocolate cookies the same way since we were teenagers.

My eyebrow raises, waiting for her to fill me in on her phone call.

She smiles annoyingly at me. Her lips and teeth are coated in chocolate. What is she... five? "Seriously, Laini. Lick your lips or something. You have chocolate covering your mouth."

All it would take is for one of my kids to see her act this way, and they, too, will think they can behave in such a manner.

She runs her tongue over her lips and teeth several times and takes a few sips of her hot drink. Then, with another flick of her tongue, it does not take her long to clear all traces of chocolate from her mouth.

"All better?" she innocently asks, battering her eyelashes. Then, instead of mentioning her appointment, she takes another mouthful of tea, then another.

My fingers tap against the tabletop, waiting for her to say something. That's it. She's frustrating. As usual, she's expecting me to ask.

I take a sip of my tea and pick up one of the remaining TimTam chocolate layered of deliciousness — a unique combination of contrasting layers of milk chocolate, two chocolate malt cookies and a cream filling of chewy caramel down the middle and coated in a thin layer of milk chocolate — take a bite, and slowly chew before swallowing.

Righto. Two can play her game. After another sip, I place my cup down and stare her in the eyes. After a minute of silence, I sigh and ask, "Laini... Are you going to inform me of your phone call? Did you make an appointment?"

She takes another mouthful of her tea, places the cup in front of her, and nods as her facial features turn serious. "Yes. My doctor wants to perform a sonogram while I am there." Really? How far is the pregnancy? "Can you go with me? It's in an hour," she mumbles the last bit while looking at her watch.

Shit. That's fast. Glad I decided to work from home today!

I watch her face change. Hairy monkey balls, she's worried.

The annoyance I felt earlier was instantly replaced with concern. "Yes. I'll be there. So, do you need to drink a gallon of water before we go?" I remember when I had my scans. I had to drink gallons of the stuff. Not comfortable at all. All I wanted to do was pee myself.

She nods before taking another mouthful of tea, then grabs another TimTam. Oh... kay. She's scared.

I get up, grab a few water bottles from the pantry, and pass them to her. "Here. These will come in handy."

Chapter Three

ESSY

*L*ess than two hours later, we stare at the dark screen with a white mass in the shape of a baby's chest cavity and watch the fast pulsing heartbeats of Laini's baby. I glance down at Laini, and we both look at one another with happy tears.

"Congratulations, sis," is all I can manage. I still cannot believe she has gone four months without realising she's pregnant. Four months! Well, eighteen weeks, but seriously... how did she not know? The kid should be kicking by now, practising Kung fu moves against her organs.

The doctor's voice echoes in the small room, and I just about jump. "As you can see, the heart is healthy and strong. Your baby is progressing fine, and all his toes and fingers can be seen. The spine is fully formed. Before you leave, I want to take blood from you to ensure everything is fine. You know, standard tests."

My happiness is short-lived upon hearing those words. I turn my head from the screen toward the doctor. "What are you not telling us?" He glances my way before looking back toward Laini.

"Mrs. Travelli, I know this is not your first pregnancy. But at your current age, we need to take some extra precautions. Plus, you should take pregnancy vitamins."

Laini nods. I can see she is becoming agitated. "Doctor, I have taken women's multivitamins for several months as I was drained and tired. It turns out I was pregnant! How did the doctor I'd seen at my last medical appointment miss the symptoms?"

Yes. How did the doctor not notice? She had looked like death warmed up several months ago and had fallen asleep on my lounge when she arrived at my place for drinks. I had never seen her in that condition before. While she slept, I went to the local drugstore and purchased some women's multivitamins containing iron. Thankfully, it didn't take much to convince Laini to take the tablets. After several weeks, she improved.

I face the doctor again and request, "Doctor, Laini would like a couple of pictures of the baby to show her husband. If he had known she was pregnant this morning, he would have been here instead of me."

He nods in understanding and prints out several pictures.

*L*aini pulls up outside my building in the drop-off zone. "Thanks for going with me, Essy."

I smile. "Where else would I be, Laini? You're my sister. I'll always be there for you." And I would. She has always been there for me. I don't know how I can repay her. "Now go and speak with your husband. I bet he will be shocked but thrilled at becoming a parent again. If you want, I can mind my gorgeous niece and give the two of you some adult time together," I say and wiggle my eyebrows suggestively. My darling cheeky niece informed me I am not allowed to use the word babysit as she is far too old now to be babysat.

Laini laughs. "Yeah, that's just the thing. That got us in this predicament in the first place."

I begin to laugh. "At least you cannot get any more pregnant."

She snorts with a huge smile. "True." She looks toward my apartment and nods. "Very true." Laini turns and leans over the middle console, hugging me. "Thanks again, and yes, I think we will take you up on the babysitting. Can you meet Emma at the school pickup?"

"Yes. What else are super fun aunties for?" I say with a laugh, pulling away and placing my hand on the door handle. Spending time with my niece is something I enjoy. I'd missed so much of her first five years and made it my mission to make up for the lost time. "She can stay at my place for a few days. You guys need this time for one another."

"Thanks, sis. Remember, I love you. Now, I better go home, make dinner arrangements, and shower. I can still feel the sticky gel drying on my skin," she says with an over-the-top shudder.

I open the car door and stand. "Love you, too. Don't forget. We have spare clothes and stuff for Emma, so we don't need to return to your place. Have fun and enjoy."

With a smile, Laini says, "I will. But this time, everything will be different. I finally have the man I love, and our family is back together. Now go. I have stuff to do and little time to do it in."

Another laugh escapes me. I bet Laini and Jaxton don't leave their house tonight or tomorrow.

Chapter Four

LAINI

My heart pounds hard against my ribs after a round of sexy time with my husband. Jax, my sexy husband, is the only man capable of satisfying my body after every session. No wonder I married him.

With my hand over my heart, I feel my chest move with each rushed breath, and a huge smile forms. A saying fills my mind: Color me rainbow colors and tie my hair in ribbons. Yep, I am one extremely happy, satisfied woman. But Gawd, I love my husband.

"Babe, you never fail to make me feel good," Jaxton pants. "Any better, and I think I'm in heaven." He rolls over, places his arm around me, and presses his tender lips to my naked shoulder. "I love you so much, Laini." His hand caresses my rounding eight-month baby belly, and I feel our baby move from within.

"I love you, too, Jax." I place my hand over his, feeling our son move against our joined hands.

"Laini, I've missed you." Until several days ago,

Jaxton has been busy filling in for one of Essy's employees as a bodyguard. "The client I'm protecting is a royal pain in the butt." Now, that is an understatement — a three-day assignment, my ass!

Jax has been away for two weeks protecting a client. An annoying rich client who is selfish.

"I know, Jax." Enough is enough. There is no need for my husband to work full-time or part-time for that matter. Technically, we are semi-retired. Thanks to my birth mother all those years ago, she placed two million dollars into an offshore account in my name before she was murdered. Thanks to her stock market skills, Essy encouraged me to invest — allowing me to increase my wealth.

"I'm sorry, baby. All I wanted was to be back home with you." That I do understand. I trust my husband. He only wanted to enjoy this pregnancy right by my side. He was determined not to miss a thing. He has been a hands-on husband — attending all appointments, selecting and purchasing the baby goods for the nursery, and painting the baby's room with stencil animal and forest themes on the walls, with glow stickers on the ceiling and walls. It looks fantastic. He wanted to do something special. He knew I could create and paint the nursery, as I have designed and painted Essy's kids' bedrooms, but something deep inside told me to allow Jax to have his chance to decorate the baby's room. I'm glad I did.

When I sensed something was wrong a week ago — A rule in our family is never to take our senses for granted. Stop and listen — They might save your life! —

I contacted Essy. Thank goodness she overruled the client, replacing Jax with two other guards. I'm thankful Jax agreed to travel to our holiday home for a couple of days of alone time together. Late last night, we returned to his hotel room to collect the last of his belongings he had taken with him for his bodyguard position, ready to leave in the morning.

Wrapped in his arms, I'm feeling slightly better being able to see and touch him. The only thing is, that strange sensation that started all those days ago is still in the middle of my chest — time to change the subject.

"Jax, I've enjoyed our time away." I press my lips to his flesh once more, inhaling his scent at the same time. "Thankfully, we are leaving for home soon."

My husband moans and squeezes me tighter. "Don't remind me of that horrid client, Laini. I've gone out of my mind and hated being separated from you, Emma, and this little guy every minute." He rubs my belly and presses his lips to my skin again, kissing my shoulder. "I do not want to miss the birth of our son."

"I want you home, Jax." I turn my head enough to meet Jaxton's lips with my own.

We've only just made love, yet my body demands more of his. Our lips fuse, and our passion increases to inferno levels. My lips sizzle from the intensity of our kiss.

His hard length pokes at the back of my thigh. I wiggle my butt as much as I can allow. Finally, Jax adjusts his body enough, reaches down to lift my leg, and thrusts forward, impaling me balls deep, filling and stretching me deliciously. We both moan in pleasure, enjoying the sensations of our bodies joining. His hips set a delicious rhythm, touching me the way I like.

No matter what position my husband takes me in, he never fails to reach all my favorite places to bring me pleasure over and over again. Each time we make love, he ensures I reach an explosive orgasm.

"Ahhh. You're squeezing my dick," he grunts as his pelvis thrusts against me. The sound of flesh slapping together echoes through the room, intensifying our encounter, causing my approaching orgasm to intensify just before it slams through me as my inner muscles begin to flutter. "Babe, I'm about to," he grunts, and I let go completely and scream my explosive release. His breath hitches as he shouts, "Ahhh, fuck! I'm cummmminnnng." I feel his cock swell within me, and he moves his hips in short, fast thrusts. He grunts, groans, and then wiggles his pelvis with his release, which sets off another orgasm within me.

The sound of a female screaming reaches my ears. Only for it to stop as Jax covers my mouth with his.

My inner muscles contract and squeeze until my body pushes his softening length out. If he keeps satisfying my body in every way possible, I will not be able to walk.

My sexy husband has accomplished another round of orgasms, and my body is more than sated — this time, I need to take a well-earned break. My boneless body requires time to recuperate, as my eyes flutter shut.

Bright sunshine blinds me as I roll over. Confusion fills my head until I realize where I am.

Jax.

I am with my husband.

Thoughts of what he accomplished with my sated body bring a smile to my face. No wonder I fell asleep. He wore me out. Yet, I savor his body and touch.

I contemplate my thoughts for the day. First, contact Essy and check on Emma. Second, let Essy know we're leaving for home soon.

If Essy needs someone to fill in as a bodyguard with her business again, she can forget about us. It's not as if we depend on an incoming wage. I receive regular payments from my successful secret writing career as a published romance author, which I use as pocket money.

There it is again. That nagging feeling keeps pushing to the front of my mind, sending my senses on high alert. Something is wrong where my husband is concerned. I don't know how or why he's in trouble. But something is coming, and Jax is in the crosshairs.

"*L*aini, are you sure you want to drive?"

I nod and smile. I've been itching to get back behind the wheel of this superb piece of sporting machinery. In another week or so, it will be far too uncomfortable to be behind the wheel. I want to take advantage while I can still drive.

Jax is eager to be home. He's determined to be there for the remainder of the pregnancy, especially the birth.

"I'm sure, babe. You can take over in an hour or so." I turn onto the open highway and put my foot down, enjoying the purr of the V8 engine.

"Okay, Lain. Just let me know when you want me to take over." He squeezes my thigh and releases a yawn.

I watch Jax from the corner of my eye as he leans back into his car seat, attempting to find a comfortable position, and closes his eyes.

A smile stretches my lips — thinking of last night and then early this morning, and scoff — I must have worn him out!

I've lost track of the number of eighties songs I've been listening to on the radio and glance toward the dash to check the time. I've been driving for less than two hours. Wow. I enjoyed singing and bopping to the music. Time has just flown, and I glance toward Jax and notice he's still fast asleep.

It's time to swap over so Jax can drive. All I need to do is find somewhere safe to pull over and stop.

I wiggle in my seat to get comfortable when a familiar buzzing pressure begins in my head.

'Laini pet.'

Her voice startles me, just about causing me to jump out of my seat.

'Girl, take it easy, it's only me,' her words caress my mind. *'I need to speak with you.'*

Before I reply, I ensure the car is safe in my lane and cruising at a steady speed. *'Betsy, what's going on?'* I scan my mirrors and then back to the road ahead.

Betsy has been part of my life since I was thirteen. She appeared to me a couple of days after I moved into the large park-side house with my then-birth parents. Betsy wanted to know why I was in her home!

Instead of freaking out staring at a ghost, I felt at peace with her and somehow knew she wasn't there to hurt me. Straight away, she noticed I was upset, and instead of being annoyed, she tried to comfort and help me.

I learned so much from speaking with her. She always appeared when I needed a shoulder to lean on. Betsy explained a bit about her past — how she was fast becoming one of the best in her field as a doctor and surgeon in the early nineteen eighties. In a time when being a female doctor was tough. The night she died, she was driving home and about to turn into her driveway when bright headlights blinded her. Another vehicle smashed into the driver's side, killing her instantly. Many years later, my birth parents fell in love with Betsy's expensive Royal Park house and purchased it.

'Laini pet, you are in danger. Please be careful.'

I check my mirrors, knowing to take Betsy's words seriously. *'What is going on, Betsy?'*

'You are being followed.'

What? As tempting as it is to look over my shoulder, it's best to watch my mirrors.

'Followed?' I don't understand. Who would follow us? *'Okay, Betsy. How far away are they, and what kind of vehicle?'*

'I am not sure, Laini pet. I have noticed two dark four-door cars following at a distance.'

Great. That does not sound good.

I knew the feeling I'd been having regarding Jax was to be taken seriously.

'Betsy, I think it might be time to phone my sister. She needs to know what is happening. She might help in some way?'

'Please, hurry, pet. One vehicle is speeding up.'

I glance at the rear-vision mirror and look for a dark car. There are several dark-looking cars behind us.

I reach beside me for my cell, press the side button, and speak my sister's name to activate the hands-free call feature. The cell rings a couple more times before I hear Essy's voice.

"Hey, Laini. Your daughter is fine."

Before she can say anything else, I cut her off. "Essy, listen. Jax and I are on our way home. Someone is following us. Two dark-looking cars. What should I do?"

"Hairy monkey balls. Are you sure… Of course you are. Look, I'll activate the tracking to follow your progress and organise a bird in the air to watch over you."

Relief fills me, knowing I can rely on my sister.

"Thank you, Essy."

"Don't thank me yet. Anything can happen. Please keep yourself as safe as you can."

'Laini pet. There. Can you see the car behind us?'

I glance at the mirror every few seconds until I know which vehicle Betsy is speaking of.

"Essy, one vehicle is several car lengths behind me.

Please, hurry. If anything should happen, look after my daughter."

"Laini, keep your focus. I want you to drive as I taught you. Now put your foot down. I have you on my screen."

"Okay, sis. Here goes." My foot presses against the accelerator, increasing my speed. I move around a few slow cars. "I hope I can delay long enough for your people to arrive."

"Please, concentrate, Laini. My people will be there as quickly as they can."

The car is right behind me. In the mirror, I see two men sitting in the vehicle's front seats. Not good. Not good at all.

Must keep moving — faster, I chant as I press my foot harder to the pedal. The speed increases as I swerve around a few more cars.

'Betsy, where is the other vehicle?'

'Laini pet, the other vehicle is racing to move in front of us. There is a side road up ahead on the left. I think they are going to cut you off.'

"Gypsy sticks, nooo."

"What? What's happening, Laini?"

Oops. I must have spoken out too loud.

"Whoever is following us is attempting to cut me off up ahead from a side road on the left. What can I do, Essy?"

"Hang on." Several seconds later, Essy finally speaks. "Laini, I want you to turn on the next road on the right. Be ready. It is coming up fast."

I spot the road at the last second, pull hard on the

steering wheel, and swerve onto the new road. The car tilts and rights itself. Thankfully, we don't roll and crash. I don't wait to see what happens next. I press my foot down to the floor.

'Betsy, what can you see?'

'It seems the car was not expecting that move. They overshot the road. They're now turning on this road.'

At least I've placed a little more space between us.

"Laini, what is going on?"

Uh-oh. Jax has woken.

"Why are you driving so fast?" His groggy voice fills my ears.

"Ahh. We are being followed." I eye the mirrors to ensure I cannot see the dark car behind me. "I am trying to place a bit of distance between us."

"What do you mean we are being followed?" His voice quickly becomes clear of sleep.

"Laini, I want you to turn... right, then... left, just up ahead of you."

"Gotcha."

"What? Is that Essy?" Jax quizzes.

"Hey, Jaxton," my sister hollers. "I wondered what happened to you."

"I was asleep, Essy," he grumbles. "Now, will you tell me what is going on?"

I tune Essy and Jax out, allowing them to finish their bantering while I keep my focus on the upcoming road signs. It's not long before the road Essy mentioned appears on my right. I don't waste any time and turn onto it, then manoeuvre my car, turning down the next road on my left.

Not noticing any roads on either side of the narrow road we're on, I call out, "Now, where?"

Essy doesn't waste time. "I want you to turn right again in a few miles. I'll let you know when to turn."

"Okay."

"Laini, if we are cut off for any reason, I want you to head for the main road. You need to be around other people. Witnesses."

"Yeah, yeah, Essy. I remember." My sister taught me well. I even became an agent on a part-time basis. My skills, talent, and knowledge far exceeded even that of my husband when he used to work full-time with the FBI. With Essy's words flying through my mind — It is always best to be in the open, surrounded by other people. Once alone — the bad guys hit.

That is just it. The situation we're in is not looking good. We've gotta get back to the main road.

Monitoring my mirrors for the dark vehicles, the sensation in my chest increases.

I think I have delayed whatever is about to happen to us for as long as I can.

"Jax."

"Yeah, baby?"

"Remember that I love you."

"I know, babe. I love you, too, but why are you mentioning it now?"

Still keeping an eye on my mirrors, I notice one of the dark vehicles getting closer.

"Essy, they are gaining on me. What do you have for me?"

"What do you mean, getting closer?"

Without taking my eyes off the road, I tell Jax, "There is a dark vehicle coming up fast behind us."

He turns around in his seat, looking through the rear window.

"Babe... I can see the car."

"Essy. Can you hear me?" I shout.

Where is my sister? She should have answered by now. No time to wait. I have to do something to save us.

I see another road coming up on my right and swing the steering wheel. "Hold on, Jax."

"What?" he shouts.

'Laini pet, don't do it.'

The car screeches as we turn. I keep pulling hard on the steering wheel onto the narrow road and press my foot down on the accelerator.

'Betsy, I have to try something.'

'It's a dead end.'

Now she tells me.

Too late.

Chapter Five

JAXTON

'*Jaxton, can you hear me?*' Huh? '*Jaxton, I need you to listen.*' Who in the hell is speaking to me?

Oh geeza. What the... Pain spreads throughout my body. The ability to move my eyelids or any part of my body fails. If I could, I would stare the annoying person in the eye and tell them to fuck off. Instead, the excruciating pain holds me in place.

'*Jaxton, for Laini's sake, keep still. Do not make a noise.*' I pause. Hearing my wife's name causes me to freeze.

If I didn't know better, I would say the voice is in my head. For now, I'll play along.

'*Who are you?*' I think with my mind.

'*Hello, Jaxton. My name is Betsy.*'

Whoa. There is that voice again.

Did she just say...Betsy? Why does the name Betsy seem familiar? Now that is bringing back a memory. My wife has an imaginary friend named Betsy.

'I am nobody's imaginary friend, young man.'

Holy shit.

'Watch your language,' Betsy demands. 'We have little time before those animals come back.'

'What animals? Am I at a farm?'

'Jaxton, stop. I am speaking of the monsters who have nearly killed you. Keeping you chained as their prisoner.'

My gorgeous wife comes to mind. We were together. Where is Laini?

'Betsy. Where is Laini? Is she alive?'

'Listen to me, young man, and listen good. I require you to act and respond as if you are dead. Laini pet is in the hospital. She is alive as well as your son. The doctors had to deliver him via emergency C-section. He is healthy and strong. As for Laini, she is in a coma. I need you to keep positive and focused on remaining alive.'

Laini is in a coma? My boy is born?

How...

'Betsy, how long have I been here?'

'Jaxton, you have been here a week.'

No. Impossible. How can I be here for a week? 'Betsy'

'Oh, no. Look, I have to go. Something is happening with Laini. I'll be back as soon as I can. Remember. Play dead!'

What in the hell is happening to my wife?

The sound of several footsteps becomes louder, followed by the clanking of keys and the turning of a lock before the sound of the door opening.

Shit. I better play dead, as Betsy said.

"Damn it. The pretty boy is still out cold," a gravelly-toned voice announces.

"Not for long. I'll zap him with the electric cattle prod. That should wake the fucker up," states an annoying voice, followed by a jackal-type laugh.

Before I can prepare my mind for the attack, a sharp poke and prod, then hot electrifying pain rips through my convulsing body. The idiot kept laughing. He enjoyed watching my body spasm and convulse, leaving his stick in one place. It is not long before my brain goes blank, and I know no more.

LAINI

Why do I feel so strange? Am I awake or asleep?

A noise penetrates my ears and turns into a rhythmic beeping. Not sure what is causing the sound, but it does remind me of a slow heartbeat.

My surroundings seem to be dark, and yet... The only conclusion I can come to is that my eyes must be closed. My focus goes to my eyelids, and concentrate on opening them, blinking a few times as my surroundings slowly come into focus.

What the heck?

What is going on?

My first impression is of a dimly lit hospital private room. The standard one bed, surrounded by medical machines. A medium-sized window on one wall — looks out onto a street. On another wall, two doors nearly two meters apart; one door should belong to the bathroom if the little lock thingy is to go by, and the other should be the actual hospital room door.

I continue to glance around — confusion fills me. Then it dawns on me — I'm standing — not lying down. Why am I here? If this is a dream, it sure is strange.

The bed in front of me contains a sheet-covered patient. Sitting hunched on their forearms on the edge of the bed seems to be a young person or a small adult. Am I meant to know the young person or the patient?

The more I watch, the more I notice the young person's shoulders shake as if they are... Sure enough, the sound of sobbing penetrates my ears. Their small shoulders moved with each heart-breaking sob. The urge to reach out, take the young person into my arms and hold and comfort them increases.

Poor thing. I wonder what is going on. My thoughts go back to the theory — this is one strange dream. My question is still the same — Why am I here?

"Momma, please wake up." Huh. If I didn't know any better, I would say that is my... "Jacky needs you. I need you. Please wake up!"

What in the world... Why is Emma asking me to wake up? I'm right here.

I shout, *'Emma, I'm right here!'* Why isn't she listening to me? This is one weird dream.

Movement beside me catches my attention just before the hospital room door fully opens, displaying my good friend Missy. Wow. Even Missy is included in my dream.

"Hey, Kiddo. How's everything going in here?"

With a hiccup, Emma quickly sits up and wipes her face before turning to face Missy.

"Aunt Missy, I thought you had left this morning?"

Where is she going? Why is Missy here in my dream?

"I'll leave as soon as I speak with your aunt Essy. She will be here soon."

Essy? Essy is arriving... Emma stands up and points to her seat.

Oh, my. I have to be dreaming. Look at my little girl. She has never been this grown-up. She's tall, for one thing! How is she so tall? Could this dream be of the future?

"You might as well grab a seat and wait. Who knows when Aunt Essy will arrive? She's always busy." My daughter frowns and glances at the floor.

This dream is weird — My sister always makes time for Emma. So what is going on around here?

I wave my arms about to see if either of them notices me. I step forward and demand, *'Will someone please explain what is happening here?'* And throw my hands up in the air, feeling more than frustrated and confused. *'I'm right here, people!'* I shout. Dream or not — shouldn't they be able to see me?

Instead of either of them giving me an answer, Missy plants her butt on the seat Emma vacated. "Thanks, kiddo. I've been on my feet all day." Missy sits back, lifts one foot, and rotates it around in circles, releasing a moan as my little girl slowly walks towards the window. Finally, my so-called best friend glances up and asks, "Emma, have the doctors said anything positive?"

I pause mid-step and glance between Missy and

Emma, waving my hands in front of their faces. Why can't they see or hear me? I fight the urge to panic. Am I dreaming because, as for dreams, this one sucks? I feel so useless. My daughter is upset, and I cannot comfort her.

Emma shakes her head, turns, and faces Missy. "Aunt Missy, I don't like the doctors here. They keep saying negative things about Momma. Can't we move her to another hospital?"

Me... in a hospital? What doctors? What negative comments? Who's the person in bed? I step forward and take a closer look at the patient.

What breath my lungs had stalls. Confusion fills me. What in the world...? My own features are right in front of me, and I appear to be asleep. I'm in bed. I'm the patient...? But how? I'm standing right here! Panic sets in. I don't know if I am dreaming...could this be real? Nothing is making sense.

The sound of a door swinging open causes Missy and Emma to stop speaking, and I swivel to see who has arrived.

Essy. There, standing in the open doorway, is my sister. I smile. *'Thank goodness. Essy is here. Finally, I can get some answers!'*

With a smile plastered on her face, Essy steps into the room. She pauses and glances around the room and glances in my direction. Her smile vanishes as she makes eye contact with me and frowns. She then glances directly at the bed and then at Emma and Missy then back to me.

Her eyes grow wide. Oh, my...she is looking at me!

'Can you see and hear me?' I quietly ask. Essy gives me a single nod. *'Is that me in the hospital bed?'* Once again, she nods, before looking back to Missy and Emma, then back to me. *'Is this a dream? As Missy and Emma cannot hear or see me.'* Essy frowns, then shakes her head and turns towards my daughter.

"What is it, Essy? What's wrong?" Missy asks.

Hang on, if this is not a dream, what is it? Because I don't understand what is going on.

Essy shrugs her shoulders, then smiles at my daughter. "I thought I forgot something important... Never mind." She then frowns at the look on my daughter's face. "What is it, Em?"

"Aunt Essy, I was saying to Aunt Missy. Can we move Momma to another hospital? I don't like the doctors here."

With a quick glance toward me and frowns, she walks to Emma, engulfing her in a tight hug before stepping back. "Emma, what has happened for you to want to move your mother to another hospital?"

"Oh, Aunt Essy." My daughter shakes her head and turns towards the bed. "The doctors are sooo negative. They say Momma will never wake up!"

'What?' I screech. Essy glances at me before turning back to Missy and Emma.

"I have a bad feeling, Aunt Essy. We should move Momma and Jack back home."

'Jack?' I question. *'Who is Jack?'*

Essy gives me a quick look, then faces Emma. "Em, I

agree with you. I think we should move your baby brother and mother to a safe location."

Huh... *'Baby brother?'*

Chapter Seven

ESSY

The last thing I'd expected to see and hear was a ghostly figure of my sister. Panic set in until I glanced at her body in the bed. With her chest moving with each breath and the medical machines still beeping with her status, I realize something else must be happening. Relief fills me, knowing she is still alive and not dead as I had first thought.

What I want to know is how and why Laini is here, appearing as if she is a ghost. Whatever is happening, my poor sister thinks she is in a dream.

I glance back at ghostly Laini. First, she has to believe she is not dreaming, and second — How could she forget she was pregnant?

What else has she forgotten?

Now back to my niece and what she said — I agree with her wholeheartedly. Even I have had warning tingles — something is not right here. It's time to move Laini somewhere safe.

I reach into my back pocket and pull free my cell. I

think it is time to speak to my parents and set the ball rolling to have Laini and baby Jack moved somewhere safer. Then go somewhere private to talk with Laini. I need to know what is happening to her.

My fingers fly over the screen, and I tap my father's name and begin the phone call.

"Essy, has something happened?" Trust my father to jump to the wrong conclusion.

I shake my head. "Dad, it is time we move Laini and Jack to the medical safe house."

"Why? What has happened?" he demands.

I turn and face my niece. "Emma has had enough of the doctors being negative and saying Laini will not wake up!"

I face my niece again and notice her lower lip trembling. Missy walks to Emma and wraps her arms in support around my niece.

"What? Why are they saying such horrible things in front of my granddaughter?" Dad screeches.

I turn away from Emma and whisper, "Plus, I'm having my tingles, Daddy. Something is wrong here."

He pauses, knowing him as well as I do. He'll be thinking of a strategy to transport Laini and Jack. "Essy, I want you to go to the nursery and watch Jack. Then, bring him back to Laini's room. Our people will arrive within the hour to transport our family out of there."

Why do I have the feeling Dad had previously considered moving Laini?

"Dad, I agree. I'm on my way to the nursery now."

I end the call, knowing my father will text me the

details. Monitoring Emma, she frowns, wondering what is going on.

"Emma, I'll head to the nursery. Jack needs to spend some time with his momma. You stay here. I'll be back shortly." I don't just look at my niece. I also glance toward Ghostly Laini, hoping she understands to remain here.

"Okay, Aunt Essy."

As I reach for the door, Missy calls out, "I'll join you, Essy." I look over my shoulder and watch Missy stand and go to Emma, embracing her in a tight hug. "Bye, kiddo. Take care."

"Safe travels, Aunt Missy. Bye."

Missy is soon behind me, on the other side of the door. She whispers, "We need to talk."

As soon as we are safely away from the closed door, I slow enough for Missy to walk in time beside me.

"Be quick, Missy. I am on a mission."

Chapter Eight

LAINI

My sister's message was loud and clear– for me to stay here with my unconscious body and daughter. As soon as she gets back, she is going to explain why I am here!

I glance back to my daughter, looking out the window, and wonder why she cannot see or hear me, yet Essy can. I wonder... *'Betsy.'* With my mind, I scream out. *'Betsy, can you hear me?'* Why haven't I called for my spirit ghost before? Surely she should be able to provide me with answers. *'Betsy, can you help me?'*

A soft, shimmering light appears to my right. Excitement fills me. I know that shimmer anywhere. Betsy!

After a few seconds, the shape of a woman appears and continues to become more solid before my eyes, even though I can see straight through her.

Thank goodness. My familiar spirit ghost Betsy heard me.

Our eyes meet, and a big smile forms on her face.

'Laini Pet, it is good to see you.' She pauses and does a double take when she notices my body on the bed. She frowns and focuses back on me. *'Oh, no. What has happened?'*

'That is what I would like to know. I don't know why I am here. I thought I was having a dream. And to make matters worse — there seem to be a lot of things I do not know or remember.'

'What...?' She glances back toward the bed and then shakes her head. *'One — you are not dreaming,'* she says with a stern look. *'Second — what is the last thing you remember?'*

I glance back to my daughter, then my body, and back to Betsy. *'I really do not know?'*

'Do you remember joining your husband for a few days and driving home?'

I shake my head. My husband–Jax. When did I see Jax? I was driving home...?

Nothing comes to mind which sets off warning bells. If I cannot remember what happened to me... what in the world happened for my memory to be blank?

I hear the hospital room door opening. The first thing I notice is the plastic crib from the nursery being pushed in by my sister. Next, the sound of a fussing babe grabs my attention. My daughter Emma steps to the side of the crib, bending down enough to pick up the baby from within. Her actions indicate she has made this move many times.

In a soft voice, she coos. "Hey, Jacky. How you doing, little man?" The babe settles and turns his head to Emma. "Come on. Let's go see Momma."

Still feeling confused about the whole situation of me being a mother again, I continue to watch Emma and the baby. Why is my mind feeling so empty?

'Laini pet, your son is handsome. He is going to be a heartbreaker.' Even though my mind is blank, I'm still mesmerized by the little bundle of joy.

All I can do is nod. *'I'll go, Laini pet. A few spirits might know something or know where to look for answers. Stay out of trouble,'* Betsy announces. Again, I nod and barely mumble *bye* before Betsy vanishes.

Emma places the babe beside my body on the bed with her hand spread over his chest to keep him in place, only for the little guy to fuss once more. If I didn't know any better, I would say he is annoyed at not getting attention from my sleeping form — typical male. Of course, Jax would pull the same face when I would pretend I did not hear him.

I move closer to the bed. I could not help myself. The baby — Jack — is gorgeous with his small amount of dark hair, little button nose, and eyes. Oh, my. So much like mine. He stops fussing and turns his head toward me, and I smile.

'Hello, little one,' I coo. I couldn't help it. His eyes widen, and his lips turn into that newborn smile, which different people comment — it's only wind. Then, he kicks out with his feet and lifts his arms. As soon as our

eyes meet, I feel a soul-deep connection with the precious little boy. He smiles, gurgles, and throws his hands about as if reaching for me.

I move a little closer with a huge smile until I hear Emma.

"Wow. I wonder what has excited Jack all of a sudden?" my daughter murmurs as she looks over her shoulder, trying to work out what has Jack so excited. The only thing she looks straight through me as if I'm not there.

I stand up straight when I realize the baby can see me. I glance toward Essy, and she shakes her head enough for me to back off.

"Emma, how about you feed Jacky? I have to step out for a minute and make a couple of phone calls."

Essy gives me the look, then towards the door, indicating for me to go with her. I nod, glance back at my children, and smile before moving for the door.

Well, color me in rainbow colors and tie my hair in ribbons. Who knew I was a mother of two children!

Chapter Nine
LAINI

I follow Essy out the door into the hospital hallway.

Before I can say a word, Essy is throwing questions at me. "No, you are not dreaming. This is real! How are you here? What is going on?" Geez, as if I know the answers to that.

A nurse just ahead of us turns and watches Essy talking to herself. Her smile leaves her face as she glances around. I can see she is trying to work out who Essy is speaking with.

I lift my hand and say, *'Hey, you're drawing attention for all the wrong reasons. Now smile and nod a few times, as if you're speaking to someone on your earpiece, then look to the nurse in surprise and point to your ear as if you are speaking to someone.'*

Essy's eyes widen, and mouths *shit* and proceeds with what I said and smiles. She points to her ear before saying, "I'll call you later. Bye." And taps her ear to show she has ended her phone call.

She waves to the nurse and walks towards a set of double doors. She glances around and heads straight for the ladies toilets. As soon as we enter, Essy checks under the four cubicle doors. Once she is happy, there is no one else in the bathroom. She looks at me with her eyebrow raised.

Okay, that's my cue. Here goes.

'Look. I have no idea why I am here. Or how I got here! I thought I was dreaming. I have no memory of this year or maybe longer, by the looks of it. I don't remember being pregnant either.'

"Damn it. That is not good."

'No, it is not,' I mumble. *'I quizzed Betsy, and she has taken off somewhere to look into things.'*

"Really!" She looks around as if she might spot her. "I wish her luck."

'So do I.' As I survey my sister over and notice the fatigue around her eyes. I wonder what she has been doing to be so tired? *'Can you update me on what is happening? Where is Jax?'*

"Argh. Now that is the million-dollar question."

'What do you mean by that?'

"Look, Laini. I don't know how to tell you this. You're in a coma. And Jax is missing. Even though I spoke to you both on the phone the day you were followed in your car. There was no proof he was in the car with you when you were found unconscious." Followed? Why were we being followed? My gaze snaps up to meet hers.

'What do you mean, there was no proof?'

"Just what I had said. He was nowhere to be found,

and his belongings were gone from your car. He has vanished. Then there is the little mystery of how your car was discovered somewhere else, from where it should have been. It was damaged, smashed beyond repair."

'The car was smashed? Were my injuries of that caused by a car accident?'

She shakes her head. "No. Not really. But they are bad, including head trauma. And yet the doctors palmed them off as if they were caused by the accident." What had happened to me? What has happened to Jax? "Whoever has taken Jax has gone to a lot of trouble to make it look like he has left you and Emma."

What in the world? Jax would never leave Emma and me. *'Why do I feel you are not telling me something?'*

"Because I am. A note was left in his hotel room containing women's and men's clothing. There was also women's hair, which did not match yours, discovered in the shower and on one of the pillows."

'And what did this note say, exactly?' Why do I have the feeling I will not like what Essy is about to say?

Essy shook her head, saying, "He does not love you anymore, and he's leaving you to be with another woman."

'What? A mistress? He left me to be with another woman?' I screech.

"Exactly. Jaxton would never leave you for a start. He loves you and the kids. He would never cheat on you in the first place. Don't forget. I had been speaking with the both of you while you were driving before our connection was cut."

What connection? Is she speaking of cell service? All right, I'm moving to my next question.

'What about our parents? What do they say?'

"Huh. Father wants to skin Jax alive, and Momma believes he's taken off."

'Didn't you explain?'

"Of course I did. I even showed her the photos you sent me just before you left to drive home."

'What photos?'

With a shake of her head, she frowns with disappointment. "You had sent me a few photos of your time together. But when we discovered your cell in the wreckage of your crashed car, your cell phone had been wiped. So there were no photos to be found." Interesting. Whoever has taken Jax is determined to make him look like he has left his wife and family.

Huh? Things are not adding up. How can my car be somewhere else? Did I crash the car, or did whoever had taken Jax smash my car with me in it?

'Can you show me the photos? It might help my memory.'

"Sure." Essy swipes her screen several times. Within seconds, several photos of the baby appear. Pictures of Emma and the baby. Our parents and the baby. Missy with the baby. Even a few of the baby resting on top of my chest. His little head was just below my chin. My heart breaks, glancing over at the photos.

When I discover who has done this to me, they better watch out! After a few more swipes, I see pictures of Jax with a very pregnant me. Okay... That answers the question of me being pregnant recently.

Essy allows me enough time to look at each picture. Then, I ask her to enlarge different parts of specific pictures so I can take in the background and any other detail I hope to jog my memory, but more importantly, in finding Jax.

Chapter Ten

LAINI

"Come on. Better head back to your room," Essy whispers as she swipes her screen off and pockets her cell. We turn back, and after a few feet, she whispers as she keeps her eyes peeled to see who is watching. "Our dad has people arriving soon to transport you and baby Jack to a safe medical facility."

'Do you seriously think my body is not safe here?'

She nods. "Yep. Personally, I would have moved you out of here two days ago."

'Really?'

"For sure. I have been keeping constant surveillance on you and the baby. So I believed you when you said you had been followed that day. Plus, I always remembered how you mentioned how you could sense something was wrong. That Jax was in danger."

Wow. Did I really say that...? Okay, we need to think of a plan and where to go from here. *'What do we need to do to protect my body, the baby, and my daughter?'*

Essy eyes me for several seconds, deep in thought.

A movement to my left has me turning. A stranger near my door has me pausing. I concentrate on watching. Who in the world was that? Hmm. If I didn't know better, I would say it was Uncle Nigel. Better known as Essy's old retired ex-FBI boss.

The sound of an incoming message has me turning back toward Essy. Sure enough, her cell beeps again. Essy retrieves her cell, swipes her screen, and reads the text. She hits a few keys in reply, places her cell back in her pocket, and begins walking again.

"Come on," she says over her shoulder. "Your ride will be here shortly. Time to prepare Jacky."

I follow Essy, moving quickly into my room — glancing around the room to make sure no one else had arrived unexpectedly. I spot Emma in the big armchair in the corner, murmuring to her baby brother as he drinks from his bottle — forgetting all about Uncle Nigel.

Emma's head snaps up in our direction and frowns. "Aunt Essy, what is going on?"

"Emma, love. Once Jack finishes his bottle, pack his belongings. We're taking your mother and brother somewhere safe. Your ride has just arrived, and guards are coming up here."

Emma smiles and looks down at the baby. "Did you hear that, Jacky? We're leaving here."

Within half an hour, the baby is fed, changed into traveling clothes, and placed in a baby carrier. His gorgeous baby bag rests beside him as he sleeps.

As for my unconscious body, Essy slowly dressed me in

loose clothing with the aid of a hired nurse, making sure not to pull any of my intravenous lines out, and quickly changed my monitor leads to a portable monitor machine. Next, I watch my physical body lifted from the bed and placed on a gurney before being covered with blankets.

Essy picks up the baby in his carrier. Emma carries the baby's bag and another bag containing clothing and a few personal possessions and follows the wheeled stretcher out of my room and straight to the nearest elevator. We all pile in, and Essy taps the basement button for the underground carpark. Her cell dings with an incoming message. She swipes the screen and reads the message.

"Damn it. What is Mother playing at?" Essy quietly mumbles to herself. "Looks like Mother changed the mission. We're headed to our parents' building."

Essy glances at me and shrugs her shoulders. Then she keeps her gaze on Davies, one of our parents' employee bodyguards. With his cell plastered to his ear, he continued to whisper into it. By the look on his face, he has just been given new instructions.

As soon as the elevator dings, the man holds his hand up. "Wait, a minute. I'll make sure it is clear and safe to proceed." After several seconds, his head pops back and encourages everyone to move.

Two vehicles were waiting for us just around the corner of the elevators. One a patient transport vehicle is ready to take the wheeled stretcher.

"Aunt Essy, can I go with Momma? I think she would like me to travel with her," Emma questions with a hopeful look. I glance back to Essy, and she looks at me, then at the bodyguard.

"Sheff. Keep my sister and niece safe." Emma smiles and does a fist pump, then climbs into the vehicle. Essy then lowers her voice, "Take extra precautions. No detours. No stops. Head straight to my parents' building. Got it?"

He nods and glances around, checking for threats. Once my body is safely placed in the vehicle, the door closes shut. The bodyguard sits in the front seat and puts his cell to his ear as the vehicle moves away. I remain in my spot, watching the van with my body and daughter roll away until it leaves my sight, and I vaguely hear Essy encouraging everyone to get a move on. I turn in time to see her tapping away on her cell... she's sending a text. Just then, she glances up, and our eyes meet.

She mouths, 'sending a text to Mom'. I nod in understanding. At least I know Essy is keeping our mother updated. She'll be expecting us soon.

Then it dawns on me. I wonder if I can leave the hospital. Shaking off mixed concerns, I position myself on the back seat and wait for the doors to close and the engine to start. So far, so good. As soon as we were free of the hospital car park, I felt a strange sensation buzzing through my body. I raise my hand, watch my fingers blur, and then come back into focus. I look up and meet Essy's concerned gaze. She, too, notices that I am fading in and out. I wonder what is happening?

Chapter Eleven

ESSY

atching Laini's ghostly body fade in and out was more than scary.

Not knowing if she'll wholly disappear and I'll never see her again scares me to my soul. The next question is, would she be able to reappear if she vanishes? Then it occurs to me a little late... can Laini leave the hospital? Oh, my gawd — can she be separated from her physical body? A bit late now!

All I wanted to do was scream out at her. But instead, my gaze snags on the other occupants in the vehicle, preventing me from voicing my concerns. The guys would think I'd flipped my lid if they noticed me speaking to myself.

As hard as I can, I concentrate with my mind and push the words from my head to her.

'Lain. Laini. Can you hear me?' I demand.

She glances up with a worried look and nods.

'Essy. I don't know what is happening?'

'Laini, try to concentrate on me. You have to focus on staying with me. Okay. Can you do that?'

She nods, even though panic covers her face. I feel helpless. The thumping of my pulse is flooding my ears. In all honesty, I'm scared shitless. I don't want to lose my sister so soon — she's only just appeared. I want to reach out to reassure her... instead, all I can do is sit here and hope she can remain here with me, as selfish as it sounds. Her features change several times. She's concentrating so hard that she looks like she is attempting to take a dump in the car. If the situation were not so scary and drastic, I would laugh.

Little by little, Laini becomes less translucent until she resembles her ghostly solid figure and opens her eyes, lifting and watching her assembled hands, turning them this way and that. Finally, her face lights up with a huge grin before our eyes meet.

Right this second, I am so proud of her. *She did it.* Laini stopped herself from vanishing. *'See, all you had to do was concentrate,'* I say in my mind with a smile. My heart is still beating double time, thinking, if Laini could not contain her body form, who knows where she would go or if she could ever return.

*R*elief fills me as soon as we pull to a stop in the undercover parking in our family building. We've made it with no other issues. Receiving that text earlier from Mother was the last straw. Laini's physical body and her son were meant to go to a medical safe house equipped with medical equipment and full-time medical staff.

Instead, Mother demanded Laini and Jack stay under her roof. Well, if she wants to take over the care, my kids will join Emma. That reminds me, I have their homeschooling all sorted. I have to grab their login details and iPads and explain what will happen until it is safe to attend school in person.

Surrounded by security, my mother appears with a huge smile. She might be hitting mid-fifties, though you wouldn't know it looking at her. The woman still resembles a badass agent, with her handgun strapped to her thigh and a knife on the other.

Before I can exit the vehicle, she is already there, unstrapping my nephew and lifting him to her chest.

"Momma, Jacky was sleeping. You know better."

She frowns at me before pressing her lips to the baby's head, gently bouncing on her feet. "Essy," she says with an eye roll. "I am his grandmother. No one is going to stand between my grandson and me. I'll shoot them if they attempt to harm a hair on his head."

Seriously... Does she think I would not take a bullet for this little guy? I have been protecting him since the day he was born. That is it. Whatever Mother has planned, I'll make sure Emma and my kids stay here. Of course, with an apartment full of kids, whatever my mother has planned will be altered. I'll make sure Daddy is here to watch over Mother.

I glance toward Laini. The look on her face made me laugh.

By the look of it, Laini is not impressed with our mother. The baby wakes unsettled in our mother's embrace. Laini moves closer to check on him. As soon as Jacky notices his momma, he stops fussing and smiles. Laini smiles back. I can tell she has already fallen in love with the little guy, even though she does not remember being pregnant with him.

It must be hard on her not knowing her own son. On the other hand, I don't know what I would do if a sizeable chunk of my memory were gone.

Chapter Twelve

LAINI

pstairs in the family-owned building, a bit of calm fills me standing inside my parent's apartment.

'What's going on?' I ask Essy.

Our mother is going off her nut and acting like her usual self when she is determined to get her own way. I would prefer her not to be clutching my son to her chest when she acts like a spoiled brat.

Our eyes meet, and I can see Essy is up to something.

'Watch and learn, sis. Watch and learn.'

Why do I have the feeling Essy has staged this?

"Essy, I will not repeat myself," our mother demands. "Baby Jack and Laini will stay under my roof. I have the room. Plus, it is quieter here than at your place with the kids." I cringe at Momma's words. If I were Essy, I would have a few chosen words to say.

No one. I mean, no one, even our mother, has no right to disrespect our kids like that. If Momma was not holding my son hostage, I bet Essy would verbally up-slap her.

"Mother, I think baby Jacky and Laini should remain here with you and Daddy," Essy politely speaks and then smiles.

Our mother is about to say something and pauses. She snaps her mouth closed and nods her head with a frown. She places her lips on my baby's head. I can see what she is thinking. Her eyes narrow before she glances back at Essy. "What are you not saying, Essy?" Always the suspicious one, our mother.

My sister shrugs her shoulders. "Just that. I've fallen behind in paperwork. My workload is heavy, and my clients are constantly phoning. I'm needed back in my office, and I cannot concentrate on work if I look after Emma, Jacky, and Laini."

My mother pulls a face before nodding her head. She turns and walks in the room's direction used as a nursery for Essy's kids and says over her shoulder, "Good to see you have your priorities arranged. Now I need to change Jack's diaper. He will be due for a bottle soon."

"Okay, Mother. I have to go. Speak to you later."

How in the hell has Essy remained so calm? I would have told mother off and removed my son from her arms. Our mother has no right to speak with us like that!

Momma walks off towards the nursery. Yet, the instinct to remain with my son is strong.

Essy turns to Emma, hugs her, and murmurs, "Stay here and watch over your mom and brother. You can sleep in your mom's old room. There should be some clothes in there you can wear."

"Okay, Aunty Essy."

"Love you, kiddo. Always remember that."

"Aunt Essy, what aren't you telling me?"

Smart kid. She senses something is not right.

"Emma, you are now your mom and baby brother's bodyguard. Keep a close watch. Can you do that for me?"

She nods. "Yes, Aunt Essy. Are you going to find my dad now?"

Essy nods. "That is my plan. I'll do my best to find him and the ones responsible for hurting your family. Now I better go before your grandmother comes back out." Emma gives Essy another hug before releasing her.

When I turn to Essy, she tilts her head towards the door and says it's time to leave.

I follow Essy out to the hall and towards the elevator when a strange thought hits me... Smell. I have no sense of smell. My mother's perfume, her standard floral room infusion candle, and even my baby — nothing. Nothing. No odor, scent, or smell reaches my nostrils. Well, that is just great. Just wait until Betsy reappears. I will quiz her with a lot of questions. Thinking of Betsy, I wonder where she is. Essy fills my vision and all thoughts of our mothers' bad behavior return.

'Essy, how do you do it? How do you remain so strong and not yell and scream at our mother? I would have gone right off.'

'Laini, our mother, can be a real bitch. Over the years,

she has done many things to piss me off. Today is not the first time she has bad-mouthed my kids.' What? How dare she!

'*Why do you speak with the woman, then?'*

'*Remember. The woman has her uses, as you might have noticed. The stick is so far up her ass she does not even realize her grandchildren do not speak to her for weeks, including your daughter.'*

Wow. What else do I not remember?

We step out of the elevator, into Essy's apartment, and head straight to her office. A new portrait on her wall has me pausing. It looks recent. In the photo, in large color, is a very pregnant me with my sexy husband behind me, his arms wrapped around me, and his smiling face pressed against mine. Wow, we look so in love. A little to the side, I noticed my teenage daughter with a huge smile holding a large sign stating. *"I'm having a baby brother!"* Sadness engulfs me. As hard as I try, I have no memory of this day.

Essy must have noticed I was no longer with her and doubles back. She looks at the same picture, smiles, and murmurs, '*You both look so much in love.'* I nod. Yes, I agree with her.

Without looking away from the portrait, I ask, '*What do we need to do next?'* Right now, I am a little confused about why we are here, but knowing my sister, she will have a plan. First, we have to discover what happened to Jax and me.

ESSY

'*Does anything look familiar?*' I urge Laini as we pull up in front of the hotel rooms where she and Jax had stayed over a week ago.

I watch Laini stare through car windows from the corner of my eye. Just by the look on her face, I can tell she does not remember being here previously. Several minutes later, with the hotel door closed behind us, I slip the room's master keycard back into my pocket as I glance around the room Laini and Jax had stayed in. Management had been told to keep room service out of there.

Men's clothing, similar to what Jax would normally wear on assignment, is scattered around the room, which is also something Jax would never do. The guy is a clean freak. Especially where his clothing is concerned. No way would he allow his clothing to be scattered on the floor.

From what I remember from the photos I saw a few days ago, something different on the pillow grabs my attention. With each step toward the bed, my brain takes in all the details, including the reddish-colored hair. A red shade of lipstick is also smudged on the pillowcase.

Now that is interesting. The photos I had seen several days ago of the bed showed no lipstick smears on the pillow. Seeing everything in person — is different from glancing at the photographs — someone else has been here since. Whoever set this room up went the extra mile providing false evidence.

Something on the floor beside my shoe catches my attention. My breath hitches as realization hits.

Argh. Hairy monkey balls. A used condom.

Eww. Bloody disgusting.

Leaning down, I notice two more used condoms on the floor beside the bed.

What is going on? Surely my parents' people would have taken photos, but then the condoms seemed to be fresh.

'What are you looking at?' my sister asks.

Uh-oh. This is going to look bad. I stand and turn. *'Um, Laini. I don't know what is happening. But. You will not like what I have come across.'*

'What is it?'

Before I can stop her, she looks down at the floor. Her eyes widen. Instead of her yelling about the condoms, she glances towards the bedside table.

I try to see what she might be looking at and thinking.

'Essy, I need you to open the drawer. I need to know if there are more condom packets in there.'

Huh?

I nod. Okay, thankfully, my sister is thinking with her agent/author brain and not as a jealous wife.

We both lean forward. Inside are LifeStyle Ultra condoms.

'Well, that answers that one!'

'What do you mean?'

'That particular condom Jaxton would never use. See how they say latex.'

'Yeah. They also say sensitive.'

'When Jax used that variety, his dick formed a nasty rash and blisters.'

I cringe at her description. *'Ouch.'*

'Yep. Jax is allergic to any latex condoms. So, I know. These condoms do not belong to my husband.'

I nod and step back, and we continue looking around the room, then the bathroom. Women's bathroom products sit on the vanity and shower. From the look of it, Jax's toiletry bag sits on the little shelf with several packets of matching latex condoms hanging out of the side pocket.

Shaking my head, I walk back out and notice Laini glancing at a few books on the small bookshelf by the bed. *'Essy, did you look at these books on the bookshelf?'*

I shake my head. *'No. Why would I?'* Glancing at the five books.

'Why? I take it you did not read the spines of these books?'

I look closer and smile when I read the third spine. *'You have to be kidding me. You left one of your books here?'*

Laini shakes her head but shrugs her shoulders. *'I have no idea. I don't recognize the title. But it has my author's name on it, though. Did I write this book?'* Her words catch my attention, and I glance at her face. I can see she is puzzled by the book. But then... Why would this book be here?

My fingers itch to look inside. The first thing I notice is the cover — one I have not seen before, even though it contains the standard half-naked man with a beautiful woman on the front. Turning through several pages slowly, skimming over the paragraphs — I don't think I have seen or read this book before — it has to be Laini's latest release or at least one of her author copies.

The more I look, the more I realize what I'm seeing. The strange markings along the inside margins appear familiar. I glance at Laini, noticing she is still busy reading the words spread over the pages. With each turned page, the markings increase, markings I remember from my old FBI days. Something undercover agents would do, leaving messages inside books for our handlers to read and pass on our information to the Director. Until I come across a full sentence of hand-written text. Neat handwriting I would know anywhere — Jax.

Another fantastic story, my love. I love your female protagonist; she has captured my heart, just like you have. All the best with your book launch. Forever yours — J.

Butterfly

I wonder what the word *Butterfly* means?

'Oh, my. It is my book. A book I do not remember publishing.'

Our eyes meet, and I can see the confusion in hers. *'Laini, do you remember writing the manuscript?'*

Laini glances back down at the open book in my hands. I watch her eyes skim over the printed words.

She nods and looks up, meeting my eyes. *'I remember writing this.'* she smiles. *'I finally remember writing this story and writing The End. But, that was a long time ago,'* she says with a frown.

'Laini... What does Jax mean by the word — **Butterfly***?'*

I watch her face as she rereads Jax's message, then her eyes widen. *'Essy, continue to search the book. There should be another message from Jax.'*

'What? What do you remember?' I ask as I turn the pages.

'It is a code name. There should be a message or something important for me.'

Wow. Okay. It looks as if Jax has been leaving messages for Laini. The question is... are they only love notes, or are they something more?

Sure enough, as I flip through the pages, I almost miss what we are looking for. I open the book as far as the page will allow. A diagram is in the inside margin.

My finger touches the sketched picture of a shell and dolphin. *'What does this mean, Laini?'*

She takes a closer look, then smiles.

'The message means the beach house.'

I wonder when Jax placed the book here on this bookshelf? Closing the book, I glance towards the door — the hairs along my neck rise.

Right, time to get out of here. I slide the book under my top and wedge it into the top of my black jeans, pulling my top over the top to hide the book.

'Essy, what are you thinking?'

I glance at Laini. *'I think it is time to get out of here and head to your beach house.'*

She nods — the urge to leave increases. We are not safe here.

I open the room's door and carefully scan the area as I step out into the hallway. The feeling I am being watched increases with each second. I hot foot it back to my car, not wasting any time.

We're both in my car within seconds, starting the engine and speeding away from the hotel.

Chapter Fourteen

LAINI

As the car enters the county highway, the wheels bounce and spin from the uneven road surface. I watch the scenery for a while as the miles pass by. It dawns on me. Nothing about this area seems familiar.

Several songs play on the radio when I notice Essy constantly checking her mirrors from the corner of my eye. What is going on? The feeling of forbidden increases. After a few more songs the feeling increases and I glance over my shoulder and notice a dark vehicle several cars behind us. Essy turns off the highway and sure enough, the dark vehicle does the same. Essy continues several more miles and we then turn onto another road and as predicted the dark car follows. It does not take a genius to work out that the not-so-subtle dark vehicle is following us.

'Essy, what is the plan to lose the vehicle behind us?'

'Hairy monkey balls. Sorry, I did not want to panic you.'

'What do you mean?'

'*Laini, the day of your accident, it had started just like this. You and Jax had been followed by dark cars. You had tried to lose them.*'

'What. You kidding me, right?'

'*Nope. While speaking with you, I lost the signal.*'

'What do you mean, you lost the signal?'

Essy made a right-hand turn and pressed her foot down, increasing speed.

'*Laini, when you realized you were being followed, you phoned me. Jax was sleeping beside you until then. As soon as possible, I began tracking you. But, when the signal was lost, something bad had happened.*'

We turned right again, taking the corner a bit sharp.

'*When my people located your car, it was not where it should have been. Someone had planted your car in a different location.*'

Who would do such a thing? '*As you previously mentioned back in the hospital I was the only person in my car?*'

'*Yes. The whole situation has been one huge setup to make it look as if Jax left you for another woman.*'

'*The one thing I do not understand is why our parents do not believe you had been speaking with us?*'

'*Who knows? They had been far too angry and concerned for your and the baby's welfare at the time.*'

Shit. Now, what are we going to do?

As far as I can remember since Jax and I got back together, we have been inseparable. I do not understand why my parents would believe he left our daughter and me.

'Essy, has Jax and I had any problems in our marriage?'

Essy turned her head, gave me a weird look, then her focus was back on the road. *'Are you serious right now, Laini? Jax loves you with all his heart and soul. Never doubt that.'*

'It's just, how can people believe he would leave his family?'

'That's just it. The used condoms, women's clothing, hair, lipstick smears, and the toiletries all indicate as evidence to make it seem real.'

The scenery flashes by. With each mile we travel, the more I look around, the feeling of déjà vu intensifies. Essy did mention I was driving around here when Jax was taken. I glance over my shoulder and notice the annoying dark car in the distance. Essy turns onto another road and floors it again.

Unease fills me. *'Essy'* She meets my eyes, then stares back to the road. *'I... I don't like this place.'*

She nods. *'It's okay, Laini. We're going straight ahead. There should be a small town another five miles away.'*

A sigh leaves my lips.

Thank goodness.

Chapter Fifteen

LAINI

The car slows and turns onto the driveway to my beach house. As far as I can tell, no one has been following us for the last hour. Finally, Essy parks her car, grabbing a set of keys from her console. With bright pink and a splash of yellow, I recognize the spare house keys I had given her a long time ago.

'Essy, someone is standing over by the side of the house. Why does he look familiar?'

She turns carefully, taking in our surroundings.

Essy frowns and shakes her head.

'Why would Uncle Nigel be here?'

'How is he here when he was at the hospital before we left?'

'What? Why didn't you say anything at the time?'

'We were a little busy. Plus, it slipped my mind until I just saw him again.'

'Another mystery to solve. Why would Nigel be here?'

Yes. Why would he be here?

Essy leans forward, reaches down, and grabs her

gun from under the driver's seat. *'There is only one way to find out,'* she says as she checks the clip before placing the gun at her back under her jacket. *'Laini, can you go into your house and check to see if there is anyone inside? Something is not right.'*

I nod and take off as Essy exits the car and cautiously approaches her old boss.

As soon as I glide through the door, I sense someone is inside my house. What the hell?

I watch the annoying man, whom I do not recognize, go through the papers on my desk. Who is he? How dare the man go through my things? He leans forward and switches on my desktop computer. Oh-no he doesn't. He's gone too far!

I race back to Essy, who is speaking with her old boss at the front door, and catch her eye.

'Essy. There is someone inside the house. He's going through my things on my desk.' She looks towards me and then steps closer to the door. *'They've turned off the alarm.'*

As she places the key in the front door lock, her ex-boss asks, "Why are you here, Essy?"

She turns the key, pushes the door open, and quickly hits my security system to the left of the door frame, reactivating it. "Why do you ask? This is my sister's beach house. I stay here whenever I want." She gives Nigel a look with raised brows. "Nigel, you never said why you are here. What's going on?"

Before Nigel explains why he is at my holiday home, the security alarm sounds, indicating something has tripped the alarm.

"Essy, turn off the alarm," he says as he reaches for something behind his back.

Before her old ex-boss can pull a weapon on her, she shoves him away, closes, and then locks the door behind her. Then, as Essy turns, she slips her gun free and switches the safety off simultaneously as she taps the alarm screen, sending an intruder alert to our parents.

I keep watch and sense the mystery man in the back of the house stepping closer to us.

'Essy, that man is sneaking up the hallway.'

She nods. *'Thanks for the heads up.'*

She quickly moves and waits for the man to appear with her gun drawn.

I move and go straight for him. I have to protect my sister. The look in the stranger's wide eyes was shock. I think he just saw me. He lifts his gun and begins firing at me.

Holy crapman, batman.

Essy calls out, "Freeze."

Instead of the man doing what he's told. He quickly turns and fires at Essy. My sister shoots a direct shot, felling the mysterious man. She approaches the man and kicks his gun away from his hand. Then leans forward to check for a pulse.

'Is he dead?'

She nods. *'Yep. Now I've done it. I wanted answers.'* She stands and places her gun back at her back. It is not long before she searches his pockets, removing his cell and wallet. Essy swipes the screen of the cell. Nothing happened.

"Looks like I need his finger or eye to access his cell," she grumbles.

Essy lifted the man's hand and tries two fingers before the third activates the screen. She scrolls through his contacts, messages, and call history.

The sound of a car screeching away catches our attention. Essy rushes to the window and peers out.

"Damn it. That was ex-boss man speeding off." The man is acting guiltier by the minute.

I turn to my sister. *'Essy, check the man's other pockets. He could have taken anything from my office.'*

She soon removes several papers and a memory USB with swift movements and pockets them. Then, she heads for the security system, turning off the noise before moving towards my office.

"Laini, I want to look at what that stranger had been searching through. We need to move quickly."

I nod, drifting into my office, and point out what the stranger had been touching and looking at, my desk and cabinet.

Standing in front of my desk, she turns my computer on. "Sis, where do you keep your cables for different devices? I want to copy this guy's cell information, including data, details, and images. Plus, we'll need to copy anything useful from his wallet, as well."

I point to a drawer in my wall unit. A place I hope still contains a variety of cables.

Essy removes several cable leads within seconds and grabs one of my sealed, boxed portable external hard drives. It does not take her long to plug a compatible cable into the cell and the other end into my desktop computer.

Once Essy has enough data copied to the new portable hard drive, including scanning the dead man's driver's license and other items of interest, she turns the computer off. Next, she stands and grabs my spare laptop bag, slipping several print books inside. Then heads to my bedroom, grabs an overnight bag from my closet, and places clothes and toiletries in it.

"I will need a cover story for why I am here. Grabbing this spare laptop and your overnight bag will look legit. You asked me to grab them when we last spoke before the accident."

I nod and look around my bedroom, wondering if anything is out of place.

'Essy, can you open my hidden safe? Jax might have left information in there.'

Essy nods. My sister had helped install it, so she would know where it was and how to open it. I hope I have not changed the password code.

It does not take her long to open my safe, which was hidden behind the wall panels inside my walk-through robe, to the bathroom. Inside are several files, an external hard drive, what looks to be more of my printed books, which I do not remember, and more USB sticks. She quickly places them inside another bag from the top shelf of my walk-in-robe and zips it up.

"I better place this bag in the car before any unexpected visitors arrive."

While Essy walks outside to her car, I remain by the dead man, glancing around the room. Different thoughts rush through my mind. What was Jax doing to cause our lives to be in such danger? Why was the dead man looking through my things? Where is my husband?

Lost in thought, I did not notice Essy appear beside me until the sound of her cell alerted me that she was back in my house. She pulls the device from her pocket, taps the screen, and answers, "We need a clean-up crew at Laini's beach house and the police." It doesn't take long to work out. She is speaking with her office. "Contact my father. Let him know what has happened and that Nigel Brenkins was here... Yes, my old FBI boss. He made excuses for why he was at Laini's house... Would you believe the man had taken off as quickly as he could when the sound of gunfire began? ...No, I don't know. ...I have to go. Yes, bye."

Essy turns her head towards me, then to the dead guy. "Time to phone the local authority on your landline. But first, I better give Trevor Bladely here back his belongings." She approaches dead Trevor and places his wallet and cell back in his pocket. Then, with a shake of her head, she returns to the security wall system, hits the switch, sounds the alarm, hurries to the wall phone, lifts the receiver, and dials the local authorities.

Chapter Sixteen

ESSY

Our father arrives within the hour with several members of his staff, along with two FBI agents.

"Thanks for coming, Dad. I wasn't sure what to expect from the local authorities. I flashed my bodyguard license, ID, and my FBI badge. The annoying part was, the immature man would not believe this was Laini's house."

"Baby girl. Don't worry. We'll take care of everything."

"Thank you, Daddy."

'*I cannot believe our father persuaded the local cops to allow you to leave,*' she says as we drive off.

"Laini, I had written a full statement. It was signed, witnessed, and everything!" I say with an eye roll. "Geez, girl. Remember, we do not have time to sit around with a dead guy and a bunch of men. We have to discover what your husband was up to. Who was after the both of you, and hunt down your husband."

The road continues to have bends and turns. Thank goodness I'm driving and not a passenger. I would have thrown up by now. I pull into a fast food drive-through and order myself some food. Once the order is available, I park the car away from several other vehicles. The aroma of the hot fast food entices my belly to grumble in hunger. I unwrap my burger and begin to eat.

'Essy, while we are here, I would like us to go through the information we collected back at the beach house.'

I nod, in agreement, while chewing a mouthful of burger. "As soon as I finish my food." I take another bite, chew, and then swallow. "We'll go through what we found in the dead guy's wallet. His phone contents and then what Jax left in your safe." I take a sip of the icy soda, swallow, reach for my cell, and turn off the location app. "I have a feeling we will find some interesting information. But I would like to know the real reason Nigel was at your beach house."

Now that is the million-dollar question. Why was he there, and what was his involvement in everything?

As soon as I finish the last of my food, I turn my cell's *do not disturb feature* on. We do not need any interruptions.

*T*hank goodness for my computer hacking skills. Laini and I cracked Jax's passwords, opened his files, and re-saved a copy of them on a coded file in my Cloud account.

'Right. From the clues Jax has left, he has been on a secret mission for the FBI and CIA. To gain intel on the mafia. The same mafia who killed my parents.'

"Yes. These memory sticks are full of files. Enough evidence to take them down once and for all. I bet this is why you and Jax had been attacked and taken, and you were left for dead."

'What I do not understand. What was Jax doing up until we were together before the accident? Was he on some undercover case?'

"As far as I know, he was guarding a problem client." When I think back to all those weeks ago and why that annoying man was determined to have Jax be one of his minders. An unknown person who became a client...

Shit.

I swipe my cell screen and call my office.

My assistant Kailyn picks up within two rings. "Hello, Boss. How may I be of assistance?"

The day I hired this remarkable woman was the right choice. Half the time, she knows what I require before I need to ask. "Hello, Kailyn. I need you to search for a client. Graham Fraide."

"That selfish client who requested Jax to be his bodyguard."

If what I'm feeling is true, there will be no file to find. "Yes. Pull the file and send it through to me."

"Directly to your email, you use on the go?"

"Yes, please, K. All the details we have."

"I'll get right on it. Give me ten minutes."

When Kailyn says she will do something, she will do it. "Thank you. Catch ya." I hit end and glance at my sister.

"My assistant is about to email me the file. I just hope all the information is still there."

'What do you mean, and what are you thinking?'

"What I think is the information I want is most likely gone if my senses are right."

'What are you sensing, Essy?'

I scan our surroundings. Not noticing anyone approaching, and take another sip of my drink.

"The client Jax was protecting, someone from my business, signed him up. I must work out who infiltrated my business and set Jax up."

'What are you trying to say? Someone went to a lot of trouble to get to him.' Exactly someone went to a lot of trouble. So all we have to figure out is, was it an inside job, or was my system hacked? *'Someone set him up and nearly killed my son and me.'* That just about sums it up.

"Laini, something I noticed Jax had contacted someone by the name of Brownsy."

'Who is Brownsy?'

"Not sure. But we're going to find out."

'And where is this Brownsy's last known whereabouts?'

"This is the interesting part."

'Why's that?'

"Brownsy was last seen at a certain bar. And we know the owner."

'We do?'

"We do! Let's go."

LAINI

ithin two hours, Essy parks the car in a paved carpark situated behind a modern-looking two-story building with a bright neon sign flashing Burt's Bar & Grill.

Vague memories of the building fill my mind, along with how the smell of alcohol would reach my nose as soon as I walked in. Relief fills me to know at least my memories are not entirely gone. Let's see if I remember the owner.

Essy opens the solid timber door to a dimly lit, sizeable area. Music plays ninety music from speakers placed high near the ceiling.

Essy turns and heads to the high-backed bar stools positioned in front of the stylish solid carved timber bar with a glassed mirror wall containing multi-glass shelving with a variety mixture of spirits, liqueurs, and racks of wine glasses. She slides onto the stool and leans forward against the long bar. A solidly built man, at least six and a half feet tall with short cropped fair hair and covered in tattoos, appears from a side doorway behind the bar.

As soon as his violet eyes meet ours. More memories flood my mind of a sensual voice as smooth as honey, with those same colored eyes and a smile to melt your panties. The only thing the vision of Braydon and myself in his bed is not something I was expecting. From the images flashing through my mind. It had been a long time ago. Wow! I wonder what had happened between us?

Hang on, did he just look at me?

"Haya, gorgeous, Essy. What brings you to my establishment?"

Essy laughs. A smile reaches her eyes as she shakes her head at the man's flirting words.

"Hello, Brayd. We need to talk privately." His head tilts to the side as his smile changes.

"What's going on, Ess?" I watch his eyes glance over to his customers scattered around the bar before turning back to me, then to Essy.

"Can we talk in your office, please?"

He nods and tilts his head in the direction of the back. I follow the direction and make out a sign stating *Manager Office*.

Essy slides off her stool and stands as Braydon approaches a middle-aged woman serving drinks down the other end of his bar. He quietly speaks with her while she slings a beer into a tall glass. The bartender pauses, glances over her shoulder with a frown, and straight at us before turning her head back to what she was doing with a nod. Braydon turns, comes out from behind the bar and heads to his office.

We enter Braydon's office. An old leather lounge stands to one side of the office. Which, if I remember rightly, pulls out to a bed. Inbuilt floor-to-ceiling cupboards fill the wall. Three gray filing cabinets behind an old-fashioned solid timber desk covered in files, pens, and a notepad sit beside a laptop and several empty coffee mugs.

Braydon sits in his office chair behind his desk, leans back, and watches me move around the room.

'Do you enjoy staring, Brayd?' I ask, not sure if he can hear me or not.

Before he can say a word, Essy asks, "Braydon, can you see Laini?"

He nods his head. He glances from me to Essy and back to me. "What is going on? As far as I know, there has been no mention of Laini's death." Braydon faces Essy again, waiting for her to answer.

"Because she hasn't. Laini was in an accident not that long ago. She is currently in a coma under the protection of our parents."

"She's alive! But how is she here right now?" he demands. "How serious are her injuries?"

She shakes her head and shrugs her shoulders. "Why Laini is in this ghostly form, I do not know." She says with a wave of her hand toward me. "As for her injuries, my nephew was delivered by emergency C-section. Laini has plenty of cuts and bruises. Her condition looks as if she had been beaten and left for dead. Yet, her car had been smashed to give the impression she had a car accident."

"Are you serious right now?" Essy nods. She glances at me, then back to Brayd. "Someone attacked Laini, leaving her for dead," he shouts.

"Shhh. Keep your voice down," Essy hisses. "Yes. That is why we are here. We are searching for the ones who hurt Laini and discover what happened with Jax."

"Jax?" He frowns, turns his head, and his eyes meet mine. "Where is your husband, Laini?"

'I don't know. Essy and I are trying to track him down. That is why we are here. We have some questions.'

"What questions? How do you think I can help?" Glad to know he can hear me.

"According to the information we have gathered, a man known as Brownsy comes here. We need to know who he is. Where he is from and what he knows about Jax's disappearance."

"When was the last time you had seen Jax?"

"That is just it. Because of the head injuries Laini sustained, she has missing memories."

"Missing memories?" Braydon repeats.

"Yes. Laini has some big gaps in her memory. On the day of the accident, Laini had phoned me to let me know they were being followed. I spoke with Jax while Laini continued to drive until her phone cut out."

"What do you mean, her phone cut out?"

"That is just it. The phone signal was lost. And not long after that, so was the GPS signal."

"What? You were tracking her?"

"Yes. I was attempting to track her to help them escape."

He shakes his head. "What a story. I'll try to help where I can."

I nod. *'Thank you. We appreciate it.'*

Chapter Eighteen

LAINI

*E*ssy and Brayd continue their banter and strategize about different people in the mafia. Names, addresses, places, times, dates.

The urge to leave the office area and head towards the bar area where the tables are seated opposite the long bar increases. The closer I approach the shadows, the more the figure of a man appears who previously blended with his surroundings.

Within several steps, I realize it is an elderly man sitting facing away from the back wall with his hand beside his ear. A dark woolen scarf wrapped around his neck, and a matching beanie hat covers his head. They were dressed in dark clothing with a dark woolen coat draped over the chair beside him. A glass containing maybe scotch or whisky sits in front of him. His hand is gripping his cell phone beside his ear, and devastation is across his face. He shakes his head and murmurs something into his cell every so often. His eyes are glassy as a tear rolls down his cheek.

Every few words carry towards me.

Whoever he's speaking with, the conversation is private. Then it dawns on me. The elderly man in front of me is the gorgeous, handsome English gentleman Dukey. A regular to this establishment. I cannot remember who he is or about his private or business life from when he was younger. But I remember he is one of the nicest men I have ever met.

My chest aches to hear his words. "No, Mae. You cannot die. Wait. I'll come back."

Oh, no. Poor Dukey. Someone he cares about is dying.

I need to do something. The poor man needs someone to be there for him and comfort him.

"Mae. Please don't die." Who is Mae? "Are your family there with you? ...What? No, Mae. How could they not be there?"

Wow. Whoever Mae is, it sounds as if her family is not there with her and she is alone. How dreadful and sad.

"I'm here for you. ...You want me to sing... Oh, Lizzy, please no. Not the Skye song. ...How am I to go on without you?"

My heart breaks to hear Dukey speak.

"Of course, I'll change the words to suit you. ...Mae, I'll stay on the line until you fall asleep. Remember, I'll always love you, my love. ...Until we meet again."

Somehow, the meaning of his words means when Mae falls asleep, she will not wake. She would have died. If I could cry, I think I would be right now.

How can one say goodbye to a loved one?

What happened next takes my breath away.

"Mary, is she ready?"

He nods, lifts his face to the ceiling, and tears travel toward his chin. He takes a deep breath. Then he begins to sing.

"Sing me a song of a lass that is gone
Say, could that lass be Mae?
Merry of soul, she sailed on a day
Over the sea to Skye
Billow and breeze, islands and seas
Mountains of rain and sun
All that was good, all that was fair
All that Mae had achieved is now done
Sing me a song of a lass that is gone
Say, could that lass be Mae?
Merry of soul, I look to the sky. There, my Mae is
    flying high.
With her wings spread wide, she glides on the
    breeze toward the stars. All that is Mae is
    now gone
May you rule the skies.
Beannachd leat, a ghràidh. Gus an coinnich sinn
    a-rithist."

Was that last part Gaelic? Why do I have the feeling he just said goodbye?

Dukey opens his eyes, meeting mine with tears, and said, "Goodbye, my love. Until we meet again."

He nods as he listens to someone on the other end of the call.

"Thank you for allowing me to speak with her."

He nods again while he listens to the other person. His tears continue to fall.

"Thank you, Mary. Remove this cell and any other evidence of my friendship with Mae before the others arrive."

He nods at Mary's words in gratitude.

"Thank goodness, Mae had thought ahead of time... ...Send everything to the usual address." He nods again... "Yes, everything. No one must know of our friendship. ...Thank you, Mary. God bless the Queen."

Dukey touches the screen and ends the call. Places it on the table along with his head. His shoulders move and shake as he allows his tears to fall in earnest.

I sit in the chair to his right and touch his arm, giving it a slight squeeze.

'I am so sorry, Dukey.'

His head snaps up, and he glances around.

"Who's there?"

I thought he could see me before. Maybe not. With the back of his hand, he wipes his face, removing his tears, and rests his head back down on his arms.

At that moment, footsteps sounded to our left.

Essy and Brayd appear.

Essy approaches the empty seats around Dukey's table and sits down. She looks at me and asks, *'What happened?'*

'His friend Mae has just died.'

'Mae? I don't remember a woman named Mae.'

'That's the name he used. Even though he also called her Lizzy.'

She turns to the old man. "Dukey. What has happened?"

He lifts his head and smiles when he sees it is my sister. "Essy girl, what a sight for these old eyes. What are you doing here?"

"Dukey, the question is, what has happened? What has you so sad?"

A sad smile crosses his face. "An old friend of mine from my childhood just passed away. Her death was sudden. I spoke with her last week, and she was feeling slightly down. She had a viral infection recently, and those annoying symptoms have remained, taking their toll on her."

"I am so sorry for your loss. What was her name?" my sister asks.

Dukey glances around before resting his eyes on both Brayd and Essy.

"My childhood friend Mae and I grew up together. We had become close through the war. But we drifted apart when she became engaged and married the man who became her husband."

"I'm sorry, Dukey."

"No. Nothing could tear our friendship apart, not even her husband. We were as thick as thieves," he says with a fond smile.

Then it occurs to me. *'Essy, ask Dukey what Mae stands for?'*

'What do you mean?'

'I think Mae is an acronym.'

'Seriously?'

'Yes. Seriously.'

"Dukey, is Mae an acronym?"

His eyes revealed Essy was on the right track. "How'd you guess?"

"Didn't you call her Lizzy earlier?"

He pulls a face with a raised brow and glances between Brayd and back to Essy with a shake of her head. "Yes, her first name was Lizzy. And that is all I can say."

Something comes to mind from my research days into the Royal family and gathering information for a historical romance writer. So that's it, I got it.

'Lizzy is short for Elizabeth. Do you know, the Queen of England's name is Elizabeth Alexandra Mary.'

'Surely you do not think?'

'Ask.'

Essy turns towards Dukey. "Is Mae the Queen back in your home country?"

His eyes widen. "You know I cannot devolve information about my past. You, of all people, should know that. Especially with your ex-FBI and military careers."

"Hairy monkey balls, Dukey."

I glance at my sister. I know there are parts of her life she has refused to discuss — especially her time in the military.

He shakes his head and replies, "My beloved has just passed away. I'm a little emotional right now. I'm sorry if I come across as abrupt."

Oh, my. Color me in rainbow colors and tie me in ribbons. Imagine if his Mae is really the Queen of England!

"Dukey, what will you do now?"

"Mae said I should live my life and go on another adventure for the both of us."

"Mae sounds like she was an exceptional woman to have around."

Dukey's lips twitch as if he remembers something before a full-blown smile fills his face.

"My girl was always so full of life. Some adventures we shared will be treasured."

Chapter Nineteen

LAINI

seless. That is how I feel. With far too many memories missing, I lack the knowledge to help and add to the current conversation.

So instead, I left them to their discussions, wandering around the bar, and studying the other patrons. The one thing I remember is that I love to people-watch. Inspiration for my writing came from people watching the characters I created after witnessing the different people and their antics over the years.

The number of patrons increases around the bar. They were laughing, drinking, and making jokes. Several middle-aged couples raise their glasses, make a toast and laugh at something the tall male bartender with short black and silver-gray dreadlocks says.

I admired the group of people watching the friendly banter between them until a woman's voice interrupts my thoughts.

'Laini, pet. What are you doing here?'

Betsy? I turn, and there, my spirit ghost is sitting at one of the other tables. *'Betsy, where have you been? So much has happened since I saw you at the hospital.'*

'Laini pet, Jaxton needs our help?'

'I know, Betsy. My sister and I are searching for clues to track him down. We now know the man Jax had been a bodyguard for has been in here.'

'No, Lain pet, you don't understand.'

'Betsy, what do you know? Where is my husband?'

'That is why I am here. Bad men have him chained in a small room. They've been torturing him. He doesn't have long.'

'No. Not my Jaxton.' Hang on. How does she know? Has she been with him all this time?

Annoyance fills me. If what she says is true, I must put my feelings aside and save my husband. *'Can you take me to him?'*

'I don't know, Laini pet. I'll try.'

'Please, Betsy.'

'Laini, when was the last time you were with your body? You cannot stay away for too long, or joining your spirit back with your flesh and bone body will be harder.'

'What are you saying... If I don't return to my body soon, I will be stuck like this!' I say while pointing at my ghostly form.

She nods. *'Laini pet, we don't have time to argue. Let Essy know we are leaving. We must hurry.'*

I don't waste any time. I rush to Essy, Brayd, and Old Dukey.

'Essy. Essy,' I swiftly say.

'Laini, we have a plan.'

I don't wait for Essy to finish. *'Betsy is taking me to where Jax is being kept, prisoner.'* Essy's eyes widen. *'He is not in good condition, and they have him chained.'*

'What are you speaking about? How does Betsy know where Jax is? Can she tell us where?'

I shake my head. *'No. she can only show me. I'll let you know as soon as I obtain more information.'*

I don't wait around. Instead, I rush toward Betsy and reach for her. As soon as my ghostly hand reaches for Betsy's, I feel an intense sensation of being pulled and stretched, and the bar and patrons vanish before me. Thank goodness I'm not in my full body, or I would throw up right about now if I had a stomach. With a jolt, my spirit form materializes, and it does not take me long to focus on our surroundings.

I don't know if I screamed out loud or not, but right there in front of me was a swollen, bloodied, bruised, and battered male who barely resembled my husband. If I had been able to breathe, I think my lungs would have failed along with my heart — the man before me. The man I love is dangling from the ceiling by chains.

Pale grayish-colored flesh appears between multicolored bruising. His nose looks as if it has been broken, including many fingers, and most likely his left leg, by the odd way it is positioned. The amount of pain he must be in.

The closer I look, the more I want to scream in anger. My husband has suffered so much at the hands of those animals. He has wet and crusted blood from his head down to his bare feet. The tips of his toes are an odd color. A shiver moves through me at the thought of all the damage throughout his body.

Thank goodness his chest is still moving. Not by much, but the main thing is it is still moving, proving he is alive. Whoever has taken him has kept my husband away from me, torturing him and breaking his bones in the process. I have to get him out of here. The people who have done this will face my wraith and face the justice system.

I head towards the only door to the room when I am pulled up short by the noise of a key turning and the sound of the lock releasing on the other side. I step to the side before the door swings open in front of me.

Right there in front of me is Essy's ex-boss. A scowl with a bad attitude covers his face, and he has a club in one hand. Right behind him is another man I have not seen before with a gun in his hand.

If I were full-bodied, I would have frozen in place. I have to do something fast. These men are going to kill my husband. I have to discover the location where we are. As fast as I can, I race past them, looking around, taking in as much detail as possible. I need to know the address. I need to stop these animals before they kill my husband.

Hallway after hallway, room after room, I continue taking in as much detail as I reach an exit door.

Without thinking, I am through the door. Out on the street. Looking left, then to the right.

Well, color me in rainbow colors and tie my hair in ribbons.

My eyes widen.

You have to be kidding me!

I know exactly where we are. My husband has been close to my physical body all this time.

'Betsy. Betsy, we need to leave. Take me back to my sister now.'

Betsy appears and reaches for my arm. *'I told you we have little time. They're going to kill him.'*

Before she says another word, my spirit body is pulled this way and stretched the other. The strange buzzing noise penetrates my ears for a brief second or two. Then, our surroundings vanish, and before I can blink, we are back at the bar beside Essy.

'Laini, where did you go? We have a plan. I have my agents headed to the last two known locations. We will find him.'

My eyes scan the area, then back at my sister, and reply, *'Essy, I found him.'*

'You found him. Where?'

'Do you believe he is a few streets away from my physical body!'

'He's what?' she screeches with her mind.

I look at her, then at the others, and nod. *'They're going to kill him. Jax needs an ambulance. He looks nearly dead, Essy. We have to stop them. Your old boss is with them. He has a weapon in his hand. We have to go.'* I'm already turning before I have finished talking. I have to get back to Jaxton.

'Laini, stop. We require more information,' she yells.

Chapter Twenty

ESSY

Laini explained the building layout and the address and gave us a rough estimate of how many people were in the building.

An old renovated factory with an underground level, where they are holding Jax, only a couple of streets away from our parent's home and my office. Who would have guessed?

Contacting my security team of bodyguards, all ex-military, and my parents' secretary to request an entire team and have them meet me at the address, less than a block away from my parents' building, asking for them to case the premises, gain as much intel, and wait for me to arrive.

Thanks to Brayd and his helicopter, sitting in his large shed back at his house, he offered to fly me to my parents' building, which contains their own helipad.

"Brayd, how long do you think it will take for us to arrive?"

"Half an hour. We have clearance for take-off."

Wow. Now that is faster than it would take to travel by car. So we'd be there one-third of the time.

"Thank you for this. I'll reimburse you for the fuel and your time."

"Look, Essy. I have always cared for Laini. I'm still kicking myself for our breakup all those years ago. She will always be the one who got away."

"Did she ever speak to you about her daughter?"

"At first, no. But when she did, I handled the whole situation wrong. I'll never forgive myself for what I said to her."

Typical male! Act first before thinking. "Brayd, what did you say?"

"I will not repeat what I said. I'm disappointed with myself as it is. Laini has every right to be angry with me."

"You are lucky she has no memory of that part of your relationship, or she would haunt your ass."

He frowns and remains silent for a few minutes before replying, "We should land in fifteen minutes."

Chapter Twenty-One
LAINI

In my brief life as a spirit, and a big thanks to Betsy, I am learning quickly to travel from one place to another without using a vehicle with my newfound skills.

All I have to do is concentrate and focus on Jaxton, and here I am. Back in the small, dimly lit room with my brutally hurt, barely breathing husband.

This time I take extra time to look at him. His face is disfigured and swollen. Where his eyes should be — is all a big round swollen mass on his head. A trail of fresh blood is leaking from the crease where one of his eyes sockets should be. Why is this happening? Why would these animals hurt you in such a way?

'*Oh, Jaxton. Please fight. Stay alive. We need you,*' I plead.

'*Laini, is that you?*'

Observing Jax, no part of his body reacted to my voice. At least his brain is still functioning.

'*Baby, I need you to remain strong.*'

'I don't know if I can last much longer, Laini.'

'Jax, please hold on. Essy will be here soon with help to get you down.'

'Ah, baby, why can't you get me down now?'

'That is just it, Jax. I am separated from my body right now. If I'm not careful, I will not be able to merge back with my body.'

'What are you speaking about? Aren't you part of my imagination?'

'No, Jax. I'm right here in my spirit form. Trying to convince you to stay alive so Essy and the others can rescue you.'

'Baby, if I don't make it. Remember that I love you and Emma.'

'Jax, we have a son. He needs a name. So, you better survive so we can name him.' I'm not about to mention he already has one. My mind is still a blank to why he's named Jack.

'We have a son?'

'Yes, Jax. We have a handsome boy. He needs us.'

'I can't wait to meet him, Laini.'

My heart breaks at hearing his words.

I wonder how long Essy will be until she arrives?

Noise from the other side of the door grabs my attention.

Oh, no.

'I love you, Jaxton.'

Come on, Essy.

ESSY

hanks to Brayd, we arrive in record time. Several of my ex-military employees met me up at my parents' building and drove to one of the side entrances to the building, Laini said was holding Jax prisoner.

"Essy, here is your earpiece and vest. I also grabbed your leg harness and guns." Thank goodness for efficient staff.

Carefully, I place the small earpiece in my ear and turn to Davies. "Thanks, Davies. Who is here, and is everyone set?"

"We've accessed local building surveillance. There are several FBI most wanted criminals inside the building, which is a surprise. And we've alerted your parents to take cautionary steps. In addition, a person of interest, Ex-FBI boss Nigel Brenkins, has been sighted. We do not know his links to the mafia at this stage."

If only these people knew half of it. When I ran into my old boss at Laini's holiday house, he had taken off unexpectedly, instantly becoming guilty of his actions. I had wondered what else he was guilty of. What is he hiding? Then when Laini mentioned Nigel was inside this building with Jax... My worst nightmare filled me with dread.

"Testing. Testing. Do you copy, Essy?" My father's voice fills my ear. What is he doing running surveillance on the comms? Who is protecting Laini's body and my baby nephew?

Not happy with the whole situation, I bite my tongue and reply, "Affirmative. When do we move in?"

"Our people are in place, Essy. We have twenty feet on the ground. As far as we have discovered, there are around fifteen people inside the building."

"Okay, thanks, Dad. Oh, and make sure there are medical on standby."

"Already on the way."

"Thank you. Jax is going to need it." Getting back to the matter at hand, it's time. "Can you switch me over to an open channel? It's time to go in."

"Roger that. You're now on our open channel."

I pause long enough to fill my lungs and find the words for my brief speech. Here goes. "Thank you, everyone, for being here. Jaxton is held prisoner at the rear half of the building. Let's go and rescue Jax. Everyone moves in at once on my command." It's best not to reveal too much information. How do I explain that time is running out for Jax, and he's severely injured? You don't, or you'll be brought in for questioning and likely face multiple trumped-up charges for treason. How would I be able to prove I am innocent and I do not work for the mafia?

My group moves in front of the dark metal door, and I give the command. "Go. Go."

We all move as one via the different doors around the multi-story building. The heavy metal door in front of me is forced open, and we rush in with our guns at the ready. The sound of multiple gunshots can be heard, as well as people yelling and screaming.

My priority is finding Jax, saving his butt on behalf of my sister, and catching the ones responsible for hurting my sister and brother-in-law.

Bullets fly hard and fast. I duck, weave and roll, keeping to the shadows with my gun in my hand and my finger on the trigger. Moving low along the dark hallway, my priority is to head toward the back half of the building. An overload of shouting and shooting fills my earpiece. I just hope no one from our team is shot or killed, I've lost count at how many hostiles are down.

The sound of gunfire increases around me. Bits of plaster and brick rain down. I rush forward. As I approach another corner, a greasy-looking thug wearing a long dark coat appears mere meters from me with a gun. I lift and aim my gun right at the stranger. As soon as I see his eyes, I shoot. A direct shot to his head. He collapses to the floor with a thud. I don't waste time and kick his gun away from his hand and continue down another corridor.

"Hostile down in the east corridor," I say.

"Roger that," was the reply in my ear.

Just as I turn the next corner, another thug appears.

This time I don't hesitate, aim and shoot. Just as the thug hits the floor, another well-dressed thug appears and rushes toward me with his gun facing me. I leap and roll to the side while my finger squeezes the trigger, shooting the man in the chest. He staggers and fails to fall. Again, I don't hesitate sending a second bullet directly at his head.

Just as I step into the next hallway, bullets surround me, missing me by inches. I double back with my back against the wall.

Hairy Monkey Balls. That was far too close.

"I require backup, pronto. Under fire," I yell, hoping someone on the team will back me up.

Chapter Twenty-Three

LAINI

With my mind filled with turmoil, I didn't notice Betsy appear beside me until she spoke my name.

'Laini, pet. We must concentrate on saving Jaxton.'

I turn to face Betsy and shake my head.

How? We're too late. They're coming.

'Betsy. I've failed.'

'Stop it. Do not speak like that. You have not failed.'

As the last words left her lips, the door flies open enough to allow Nigel inside the room, followed by a man I did not recognize.

I hear Betsy make a noise. Her ghostly form pales more than her usual color. From the look on her face, she knows the man.

'Betsy, what is it?'

Nigel curses and demands the stranger to shut and lock the door.

'Betsy. Speak to me.'

'Laini Pet, I know that man. He was my fiancé.'

'Your what?'

'Johnny was my fiancé from before I was killed.'

'Who in the hell is Johnny?'

'Johnny comes from a family of mafia men. He was the second youngest of five brothers. Johnny wanted nothing to do with the mafia. He was planning to leave the family business for good.'

'Hang on. After all the years we have known one another — this is the first time you mentioned you had a fiancé from a mafia family?'

'Over the last few years, little by little, flashes of lost memories have been returning to me. When we met all those years ago, my only memory at the time had been of where I lived and that I was a well-respected doctor and surgeon working at the local hospital.'

'And since then?'

'Well, since then, vague memories of the local mafia and how they had wanted to purchase my house have surfaced, and that I refused to sell. When I go back over that night, I keep seeing bright car lights coming straight at me when I am turning into my driveway, and something hard smashing into my car. Next, I wandered around in my house, discovering I was dead. I'm not sure how much time had passed when I met you at my house.'

'So, does that mean your fiancé wanted your house?'

'No. I don't think so. It was his father.'

'His father?'

'Yes, his father. The mafia boss. He is the leader of the Apolo Syndicate. The same people who had come into my home slaughtered your parents and burned our house to the ground.'

'*No.*' I shake my ghostly head as the memories force their way through my mind. No. I don't want to relive it again. Images as a teenager at Essy's house when her parents returned from work early, informing me the syndicate had murdered my parents, and we had to leave before they found me.

It looks like they found me after all those years.

Focusing back on the two men, I listen to their hushed voices. "Nigel, we have to get Jaxton out of here. One of my father's men will arrive before we know it and kill him."

"I agree. Remember, they must never discover who we are."

What is Nigel speaking about?

"Come, help me unchain him. I grabbed da-key."

"Thank goodness. We must hurry."

I watch Johnny reach into his front pocket and remove a solid silver key.

At least I know there is a key to unlock Jaxton's chains. Nigel grabs the chair on the other side of the room and places it beside my husband.

It does not take the two of them long to release Jax from the confinement of the chains.

Just as Johnny attempts to lift Jax from the hooks the chains are attached to, he glances up and notices Betsy and me with wide, shocked eyes, as Nigel places Jax on the chair.

His complexion pales, and his mouth opens and closes.

"Betsy... is that you?"

How can he see us?

I watch Betsy nod. *'Yes, Johnny.'*

"Oh, my god. Your... Your... dead. How can this be? How can I see you?" His focus turns to me. His features change even more. "Isn't your name Laini? Last I heard, you were still alive. How are you here? Have you died?"

First, I glance at Betsy, then at Johnny. *'As far as I know, my body is still in a coma. I have been searching for my husband.'* I look at Jax, slumped and barely breathing. *'And I found him.'*

"We are not da-bad guys here, Laini. We're here to rescue Jaxton and get him out of here before one of da-Apolo Syndicate men bursts in and shoots Jax."

'How do we know you're telling the truth? Can we trust you?'

The sound of gunfire increases on the other side of the door. We are running out of time. It's times like this I require Essy by my side.

Chapter Twenty-Four

LAINI

Surprise is an understatement when I watch Nigel and Johnny carry Jax through a hidden door in the wall paneling. Relief fills me, watching Jax being removed from the prison he has been kept in as fast as they can. Then, both men trudge down a secret narrow hallway, which I discover leading to the outside, where a van is waiting.

Then it occurs to me. Essy is here to rescue him. Uh-oh. I don't waste any time and rush to find my sister to give her an update on what is happening. She needs to know Jax is on the move.

Improving with my new skills, misting I reappear by Essy's side only to find she was busy returning fire, shooting at several bad guys, and avoiding being shot. I weigh up the situation. One guy in a suit comes at her from her right, just as another creepy-looking man attempts to sneak up behind her with another not far behind him.

'Essy, shoot the guy sneaking up on your right.'

She pauses but doesn't say a word and follows my advice — a direct headshot to the man on the right.

'*Two behind you.*'

She spins and fires. Both men go down in a slumped heap.

She gives me a nod of thanks before I remember why I am here. '*Essy. Nigel and a man named Johnny have removed Jax from the room he has been kept a prisoner in.*'

'*What? Nobody has left that room as far as we know.*'

Well... she is going to be surprised when I explain how. '*They escaped via a secret door in the wall paneling. Down a narrow passageway leading outside, straight to a waiting van. I must follow them.*'

'*Go. I'll be fine,*' Essy yells over her shoulder.

The last thing I see is Essy rushing toward the room where Jax is kept as I disappear from the building and catch up with unconscious Jaxton in the back of the van. Nigel was leaning over Jax, checking on him. As for Betsy, she's up next to the front seat, speaking with Johnny, who is driving.

'*Johnny, I want to know... Did you have anything to do with my death?*' Betsy demands as the van races down the road heading towards the freeway.

Johnny glances over his shoulder, then towards the road, followed by a quick glance in the vehicle's side mirrors before returning to the road.

"Betsy, I loved you with my heart and soul. I had tried to save you."

She shakes her head. '*Whatever you reckon. The last*

thing I remember is seeing headlights, the sound of crunching metal, and pain, then nothing.'

Oh, my. Betsy is annoyed. I don't think she believes Johnny.

"*B*etsy, my love. The night of your car accident was no accident at all. Because I refused to join the family business, my father took control of my life by removing you for good. Little did they know you had survived the crash. With the help of a couple of my own men. You were removed from your vehicle and rushed to a private hospital, where you stayed until our daughter was born."

'*What do you mean, our daughter? I was never pregnant. Hang on. Until our daughter was born?*'

"That is just it, Betsy. We were secretly married with a child on the way. We were due to leave the U.S. and travel to Europe to live. But it was not to be. You were on life support. A coma I was told you would never wake from. Mysteriously, you held on until the pregnancy reached eight months, then your body gave up. Our daughter was born by emergency C-section, and you sadly died in my arms, with our daughter by our side. I sneaked our daughter to a young couple I trust and to be raised as their own."

I watch Betsy become excited at the realization she is a mother. Something she has always wanted. '*Where is our daughter? Is she safe? Is she happy? Has she achieved any life dreams?'*

"She is safe. Our daughter is extremely intelligent, like her mother, and has a successful career in advertising. She's married and recently had a baby boy. I named her after your beloved grandmother."

'My Grandmother... Do you mean our daughter's name is Francine?' Betsy says in amazement.

Johnny smiles and nods. "Yes, Betsy. I wanted her to have something special from you."

Oh, my. I cannot believe it. Betsy was married and had a family. Hang on. Why does that name sound familiar? Francine in advertising? I wonder if she is the same Francine working for Missy here in the U.S.? Wow. If she is, what a small world.

I glance toward Nigel. It is my time to ask questions. I need answers and want them now. *'What about you, uncle Nigel? Why were you at my beach house? Why have you been working with the mafia?'*

Nigel looks up from Jax to me, then back to Jax again. "Laini, I have been undercover for a long time. Only a selected few know the truth."

'Do my parents know the truth?'

"Your father does. Only because he discovered my association with the mafia after your accident."

'My accident. I was hurt and left to die. Were you there? Did you have any part in what happened to Jax and me?'

"No, Laini. I was not there. I was told to go to your holiday house as a lookout. Trevor Bladely was there to collect information and destroy any evidence. Instead,

Essy arrived and shot him. Preventing the destruction of your house."

'I was there, Nigel. Who do you think told Essy to go into the house and activate the other alarm? I had seen your spy in my office. I did not appreciate seeing someone going through my belongings.'

"You were there?"

'Yes.'

"For the record, Laini. I am sorry for everything which has happened. You should not have been hurt. It goes to show the mafia did not care that you were pregnant. I'm amazed they kept you alive." He's amazed! Unbelievable. How dare he say something like that?

'Nigel, those animals are the same people who killed my parents. They are the ones responsible for me going into long-term protection.'

"Yes. I know," he replies. "Which is another reason I was placed in long-term undercover work. The Apolo Syndicate had to think I was a part of them. It had taken a few rules to be broken to have you pronounced dead. A dead homeless female was placed in your parents' house. You were known to the Apolo Syndicate. To keep you alive, it had to look as if you were killed and all loose ends are taken care of."

Oh, my. The number of years to be working undercover...wow.

'What I would like to know, why did you remove Jax when my family was about to save him?'

"They would not have escaped from the building with him. So we had to do something. It does not help when they have a secret agent working against them. Plus, knowing Essy, she would have followed us via the secret exit before the building blew up. Saving her life."

'What?' Blows up! My sister. She could be dead! No. Surely not. I lean in closer towards Nigel. *'The building is going to blow up, and you're only informing me now. I have to warn her. Warn the team.'*

I didn't wait to listen to what Nigel was saying before I disappeared and mist right next to Essy. She had left the room Jax was held prisoner in and started towards the main part of the building when I saw Daddy approaching her.

'Essy, grab Daddy. Danger. Leave. Now.'

'What are you saying... Danger? Where?' She glances all around.

'Explosion. Exit the building via the secret tunnel. Hurry before you run out of time.'

She knows to trust me. And thank goodness this is one of those times. Daddy gives her a strange look before she grabs him and calls out to team members nearby.

"Danger. Code purple."

"What is going on, Essy?" he says as he glances around.

"Daddy, move. No time to look around."

"Essy, how do you know?"

"Move. Faster, everyone," she yells.

Essy continues to double back and go into the room used as Jax prison. I lead the way to the secret panel.

"What the hell. Essy, we have to gather evidence."

Daddy pulls back when he notices the room Jax was kept in.

"No. The building is about to explode. We have to get out."

"You've led us to... Oh, my god. Look at all the blood. And those tools."

"Dad, focus." As they reach the secret open panel, several explosions begin to shake the building. "Quick. Run," she shouts over the noise.

Essy grabs our father's arm and pulls hard as she takes off. As fast as they can go along the long, narrow escape passage. Debris and dust begin to rain down around the group.

'Keep moving, Essy. Don't stop.'

'Hairy monkey balls, Laini. I'm moving as fast as I can go.'

With her hand over her mouth. My sister coughs from all the debris dust. She reaches the end of the narrow hallway, kicks against what appears to be a door, and keeps moving away from the building.

One by one, the group exits the falling building. Covered in particles from the falling building, and stands in the open street, coughing.

'Essy, keep moving. You are being watched. Be careful. There's a spy amongst you.'

'Are you sure?' She glances towards me, then nods. *'Of course, you are.'*

She continues to walk and wipes her face with the inside of her top.

'Essy, you must know. Nigel is a long-term undercover agent. He says he is on our side. Johnny from the Apolo

Syndicate is an undercover government agent. He was Betsy's husband. It was his family who had murdered Betsy and my parents.'

'What? Are you certain?'

'Very. Look. Jax was going to be killed, which is why Johnny and Nigel escaped with him. They are taking Jax to a private hospital for treatment. I must go back. I need to be with him.'

'Yes. Go. I'll remember what you said. There's a spy amongst us. Keep me updated.'

'I will. Now be safe, Essy. Luv ya.'

'Luv ya, too.'

ESSY

My sister vanishes before my eyes, and I gasp. That is one sight I will never adjust to. I never want to see my sister disappear like that again. We must work out how to place her ghostly spirit form, or whatever she is now, back into her unconscious body. Sirens and alarms blare and screech around me as I cough, trying to clear my lungs from the dust and debris particles.

A shadow appears in front of me, and I glance to my left, straight at a pair of what used to be black colored boots. Now they are coated in thick dust and debris.

"Essy, are you okay?" My father splutters and coughs. Once he controls his breathing, he wraps his arms around me. "Where is Jax?"

Without thinking, I pull the earpiece out of my ear, show my dad, and then shove it deep into my pocket. He quickly follows suit. While my father's ear is beside my head, I whisper, "What I am about to say, keep to yourself."

"Shhh. Make sure no one can hear you," Daddy hisses. Then, he lifts his head to see if anyone is listening. Then removes his earpiece, and I quickly do the same.

Yes. I gathered my father knew about the undercover agents. I want to know why he mentioned nothing to me. Especially when my brother-in-law was deep in trouble, and dad never did a thing to help Jax. "Jax was removed moments before the explosion by Nigel and a secret undercover government agent, a Syndicate Apolo family member, Johnny."

"Come on. We have to get out of here." Dad announces. "We'll go back to the office." I knew he was speaking about going back home.

"Dad, there is a spy in your group. At the moment, I haven't worked out who it is. I first thought it might have been Nigel," I whisper.

"Come on, Essy. Time to move. Your mother is waiting for us," he says louder. "Let's head to the SUV." From the look in his eyes, it changed when he mentioned Mother. I'll play along for now.

Before I take a step, Brayd approaches me from the crowd of onlookers. "Essy, I was worried about you. When the building started...yes, well, I'm not sure where I should be?"

I nod. I had forgotten he was waiting outside the building. He didn't appreciate being told to remain outside while I went into the building without him. Near my father's SUV, I said, "Brayd, come on. I'll introduce you to my dad as we walk." My old friend nods and gives me a strange look before glancing around. I bet he is looking for my sister — Brayd steps beside me as we walk toward the side of the SUV. "Laini is watching over Jax," I whisper. "He was secretly taken to a private hospital."

With a quick sharp nod, he stops beside the SUV and eyes my father.

"Dad, I don't know if you remember Braydon. Thanks to him, he flew me back here. It's his chopper on the helipad."

"Thank you, Braydon, for flying Essy here."

"You're welcome. If I can assist with anything else."

Before he can say anything else, my father quickly says, "Just remove your chopper from my helipad. Essy's husband is due to fly in later this evening."

"What?" I demand.

My dad nods his head. "Your husband had a meeting this morning and used his helicopter to attend the meeting over two hours away. Dekk didn't want to waste time in traffic."

Knowing my husband, he hates driving in heavy traffic. He would prefer to fly than have his driver, Edwards, drive him. Plus, with me being away, he would have made sure our kids were safe in our parents' penthouse. Thinking of my gorgeous children. I wonder what they're doing?

Dad opens the driver's door.

"I get it," Brayd says. "I'll leave as soon as I get clearance."

"Thank you, Brayd." I glance toward dad and notice his eyebrow raised. I raise one of mine back at him. Dad was not happy that I used his helicopter landing pad on the roof and turned back to Brayd. "Dekk and I appreciate your thoughtfulness."

Brayd nods in reply. He turns and lifts his cell to his ear and begins speaking to someone regarding a flight path.

Before I can climb in, someone yells out my father's name. We pause before turning around.

"Jason, wait up a minute," a stranger I do not know hollers, and my father stiffens. My fingers twitch beside me, slowly reaching for my gun.

Then, my father whispers through clenched teeth, "Pass me your earpiece. Then take the SUV back to the apartment. Chances are I'll be stuck with these guys for a while."

I whisper back, "Keep safe, Dad." And slip my earpiece into his hand.

"Always."

As my father turns, he faces the stranger with a fake smile.

"Stevenson, is there something you require?"

"Yes. We noticed you removed your earpieces. We tried to speak with you." My father glances towards me, then at Brayd, and back to the stranger named Stevenson.

"We didn't realize we were still needed."

Stevenson nods. "We require you to assist us in gathering and questioning the men we have captured today."

Dad nods and turns towards me.

Taking the hint, I step forward and hug my father. "Dad. We better not keep you." He slides his hand into his pocket to retrieve his earpiece, adding it to mine in his hand. "I need to take Brayd back before we miss that meeting."

Dad nods. "Then take the SUV back. I'll catch a lift back later." He then reaches out with his right hand towards Brayd.

My friend caught on quickly and plays along, shaking my father's hand. "It was a pleasure to meet you, Jason." Brayd turns to me and says, "We better go, or we'll be late." I give him a slight nod before he opens the front passenger door and climbs in.

I nod and say over my shoulder as I walk to the driver's door, pulling it open. "See you later at dinner, Dad." Then I climb into the driver's seat, start the SUV, and drive away.

As soon as I turn the corner, Brayd asks, "Do you need me to hang about?"

I shake my head. "*No*. Thanks for asking, though." And turn into the next street along. Pity things did not work between Brayd and Laini. But, then, her heart always belonged to Jaxton. The man beside me is ex-military. If only he could find the right woman to settle down with. Until that day comes, he'll continue to be a non-relationship type of guy. "Unfortunately, everything is back on hold until I know what is happening with Jax."

He nods, and I concentrate on driving. It isn't long, and we're parking in my parents' building garage. We exit the van. I'm stuck between walking to the apartments' elevators or the ones for the roof.

"Essy, can you walk me to the roof?" Well, that

answers my question. I nod to Brayd and point at the elevator to our right.

"All right. I'll show you the way."

From the corner of my eye, I can see that Brayd seems to be struggling with something on his mind. I remain silent and wait for him to speak.

He glances back at me and then asks, "Is Laini's body..." he looks up with a tilt of his head toward the ceiling, "is she here?" Indicating the floors above us.

"Yes," I say and nod. "It is safer for her to be here than in the hospital. Especially with the Syndicate people still out there."

"Wow. I didn't realize her life was still in danger."

"My sister and her children are all in danger."

"Children?" he says with a frown. "...That's right. Laini was pregnant with her second child."

"Yes. Her children mean the world to her. Well, her daughter does. Laini has no memory of her son or the last several years or more," I say.

"You're serious. Still, no memories."

"Sadly, yes," I murmur and face him front on. "One major problem is — to figure out how to get her spirit form back into her body."

He lifts his brow in thought. "Now, that is one thing I know nothing about." He pauses for several seconds, then smiles. "I think I might know of someone who might. I'll discretely make some inquiries and contact you when I find out something."

It would be fantastic if Brayd is successful. We need to discover the answer to place her spirit back into her body. "Thank you, Brayd. That would be great."

We step out onto the roof area facing the helipad.

"I better go," he says. "I really cared for Laini. I was a fool for acting the way I did."

"Brayd, remember, Laini has always loved her husband. You guys would not have lasted."

"I figured as much. But a guy can dream."

"Thank you again for flying me out here. Send me an invoice for the fuel and any other expenses."

"Anytime, Essy. Anytime."

Just as he goes to say something else, his cell rings.

He removes the device from his pocket. Mutters, *"Dammit. What now?"* He looks up at me and says, "Sorry, I have to take this." He steps away from me and answers the call. "What?" he demands and continues walking, checking on his helicopter as he listens to the caller. I can see he says several words back. He shakes his head. Then nods and replies. He glances at his watch and nods, and says something else. He then ends the call, turns, and walks back towards me as he slips his cell back into his pocket.

"I have to go. An emergency has come up. Let me know if you need me."

I nod. Not sure if I should involve Brayd anymore than he already is and say, "I'll call in and see you soon when I pick up my car."

"Make sure you do, Essy. Until next time," he says with a wave.

I watch Brayd sit in his helicopter, place his headset on, and prepare for liftoff. Finally, the chopper blades begin to move, and I step closer to the handrail next to the roof access door until the blades continuously spin.

The wind from the spinning blades causes my hair to fly about my face until I reach for it and hold it in place. Before long, he waves, the helicopter lifts, and I watch Brayd fly away.

With my husband away, my kids usually spend time with their grandparents, meaning they should be somewhere in my parents' penthouse apartment. I go to my old room and change into clean clothes, I still keep here. From there, I head down to the theater room. The sound of laughter tickles my ears, causing me to smile.

I quietly opened the door a fraction. There dancing before the large wall-size tv screen is Em, dancing about with Frazer, Bella, and Byron.

My young daughters' favorite movie, Anastasia, splashed across the screen. The character's voice booms throughout the room's surround speakers. My gorgeous little girl Bella is pretending to be Anastasia, singing, *Once upon a December*. Her brothers and Emma dance around her, pretending to be the other ballroom dancers.

Just as Bella finishes belting out, *Across my memory,* making sure she stretched the word memory out on the top of her longs, she glances up towards the door and spots me with a huge smile.

"Momma. Look, Momma is here."

Emma pauses the movie, and my kids race toward me as I open the door wide with a smile.

"Hello, my gorgeous ones." My little girl races into my arms, and I lift her high onto my hip. My twin boys wrap their arms around my waist.

"You're back. Can we go home now?" my son, Byron, asks.

I meet my son's gorgeous eyes, which match my husband's, and shake my head. "Not yet. I need you, your brother, and your little sister to remain here with your grandparents. So I only stopped by to check on you guys."

"Come on, Mom. Why can't we go back to our house?" Frazer demands.

No. Are my thoughts on the matter.

My son has become a little too busy on his computer, spending time online with people he says are his friends. From what I have so far discovered, two are indeed his friends. The other people I have since discovered are not his friends at all. I have had to block several cyber-attacks on our computer systems. Over the last month, I selected two top IT specialists to track these potential criminals down. Whoever they are, I have had enough of them encouraging my son.

"Look, kids, your father should be back soon." Thank goodness my parents have Rosely, who comes in and cooks several times a week. I wonder if she's rostered on tonight? "We'll all have dinner with Grandma and Granddad. Then we'll go home for the night."

Byron gives his twin the eye. If I didn't know any

better. It was the look to behave. My little man is the one who takes control of his brother. He is a lot like Dekk. But at the same time, he has many of my qualities for adventure and also a thirst for learning and improving his skills. At times, Frazer reminds me of his uncle Leo. A head for trouble. One thing is for sure. We will have to break him out of this habit. I do not want to lose my son.

"Hey, guys, how about you continue watching the movie, and I'll check on our new little family member. I bet Jack is waking up wanting his diaper changed. Unless one of you would like to do it instead?"

The three older children all said, "No." Little Bella nods. I smile at my young daughters' innocence. What until she comes across a smelly diaper — she'll never agree to change one ever again.

"Go on, go sit down. I'll go to Jacky. We'll catch up later, okay?"

"Yes, Mom," my kids say in unison. I look toward Emma, and she nods and smiles at me.

*M*y heart melts when my baby nephews' eyes meet mine.

"Heya, little man. Soon you will have your momma and daddy back home where they belong."

I swear he smiles at me before taking the nipple back in his mouth and continues to drink from his feeding bottle. It is not long, and his bottle is finished, and he's fast asleep in my arms.

With his little head against my shoulder, he deeply sleeps, holding my blouse tightly in his small hand. If I am not careful, I will become clucky and want another little one — time to place this little guy back in his bed.

Just as I turn to walk out of the room, I nearly jump out of my skin. Right there, staring at the baby is my sister. *'Hairy monkey balls, Laini. Warn a person next time.'*

'Sorry, Essy. I was caught up looking at the baby. I cannot believe he is mine.'

'Get used to it. He's all yours and Jaxton's.'

I walk through to the other room, where her body is, and spot mom sitting beside the bed reading a magazine until she looks up, meets my eyes, and smiles.

"Essy, good to see you. How has everything been going? What have you found out?"

Not sure how to answer her, I step closer to the bed and reach for Laini's physical hand, giving it a slight squeeze.

"How is Laini doing?"

My mother frowns, turning her head to look at Laini.

"There is no change. Emma thought she saw Laini's finger twitch, but no one else had seen anything."

"Really? I hope she is right. We need some good news."

"Why?" my mother asks. "What happened at the warehouse?"

I shake my head in reply. I have to be careful how I

explain things. "As I said, Jax was taken all along, and someone had gone a long way to make it look like he was cheating on Laini. Instead, he was being kept prisoner and tortured. I will track him down, and I will bring him home when it is safe."

"I am so sorry, Essy. But all the photos... I had seen, and the evidence was overwhelming."

"It is a pity you did not believe me in the beginning. We might have discovered Jaxton before now."

She shrugs her shoulders. "Yes. Now that was a shock. He was under our very nose."

Unbelievable. And my parents used to be one of the best working FBI teams. I wonder what had happened to them to fall so far!

I am still annoyed with them. They should have believed me in the beginning. But, no. They wanted to believe the fake proof. I say it again — Unbelievable.

I glance towards Spirit Laini as she shakes her head. She's thinking the same thing as me. Our parents are frustrating and annoying, who only believe what they want.

Chapter Twenty-Six
LAINI

$\mathcal{I}$f I could speak out loud, I would yell at my mother.

Okay, time to speak with Essy.

I indicate for her to leave the room, and she gives me a quick nod in acknowledgment.

"I have to go, Mom. I'll be back later," Essy says as she walks through the doorway.

"Oh, bye, Essy, Love."

'Let's go downstairs to your office,' I say.

She nods in acknowledgement.

$\mathcal{E}$ssy sits down behind her desk, looking over messages and emails on her computer. A few minutes later, she finally looks up from the screen.

'Laini, have you remembered anything?'

Good question. I haven't had time to think about anything.

'I have no idea?'

She nods at my words. *'Okay, do you remember where you were married? Writing your last book, where you were when you discovered you were pregnant.'*

What a strange bunch of questions.

She raises her brow and waits for me to reply.

I stand there by her desk, thinking of my baby boy. Focusing. Trying to remember anything about being pregnant. Nothing. Next, I think about Jax. Now that I think of it... where did we get married? Then there is my writing. What is the last book I wrote?

Nothing is coming to mind. Nothing.

I glance back, meeting Essy's eyes, and shake my head.

'Nothing. What am I going to do?'

Essy stands and approaches me. *'If I could hug you, I would. But, for now, concentrate on Jax and getting back into your body.'*

I nod and turn away from her. *'Essy. There is something I need to discuss with you regarding Jax.'*

'What is it? Has something happened?'

I spin around and see the worried look on her face.

'No. He's still alive,' I squeal, *'But...'*

'But what?'

'I think it might be best until the spy is caught to leave Jax where he is.'

'What?'

'Look, don't get me wrong. I trust you. It's just.'

'Just what? Keep his whereabouts confidential. But I wouldn't tell anyone.'

'I know that, Essy. But... we do not know who the spy is? Where they are.'

'I will not change your mind, am I? What happens if anything happens to you? How will we find him?'

'Betsy will let you know.'

'Betsy? Is she still around?' Essy glances around the room.

'No. Yes. I mean, she is still around, but she is back with Jax. Plus, I think it will be best to use that box thingy to search and check for bugs, etc. You never know who might be listening to your phone calls, emails, conversations, here or anywhere.'

She nods at my words.

'Don't worry, Laini. That is another reason why I came into my office. I keep one in my wall safe, so I know it has not been tampered with and is safe to use.'

'Good call.'

She smiles. 'I thought so.'

Chapter Twenty-Seven

LAINI

*E*ssy was efficiently searching her office, home, and her private car, which she keeps downstairs in the parking garage. She also checks electronically all her computers, her internet modem, her cell phone, and even her home network — everything which requires internet access.

She came across eight physical bugs. And ten program bugs in her electronic system for her home, office, and building security.

Because of her knowledge of computers and programming, she soon removes them, but not before inserting a piggyback system to track who was monitoring her.

Within twenty minutes of tracking, whoever was monitoring her has now put an end to their electronic surveillance.

With her quick thinking, she narrows the area down to where the hackers are situated.

I left her to go back to my physical body to check my

status. With no known changes, I misted back to Essy in her office, arriving in time to overhear her plans. With two of her most trusted security team members as they prepare to leave.

'Laini, good. You're back,' she says as soon as she spots me by her door. '*As you can see, we're about to leave. I've organized a reconnaissance mission. While there, I'll return the favor to the hackers. Once we're finished, we'll swing by Brayd's house and pick up my work car.*'

'*Sounds like a plan to me. Make sure to say hello to Brayd for me.*'

Essy frowns. '*What do you mean? You can tell him yourself!*'

'*No, Essy. I am staying with Jax. I need to be with him.*'

'*Look, Laini. I understand where you're coming from, but I would prefer you to be with me.*'

'*Essy. Come on. You do not need me at your side 24/7.*'

'*Laini...*'

'*No, Essy. My husband is close to death. So I am staying with him.*'

The glint in her eyes turns hard. '*If anything happens to Jax, you better not join him and abandon your physical body forever. Your kids need you. Always remember that.*'

Wow. Essy is not mixing her words.

'*Look, sis. I love you. But, I also love my husband. My choice is to be by his side and encourage him to live.*'

'*Oh, Laini. I'm being selfish, aren't I?*'

'*I know you mean well, Ess. Of course, you want to*

find the people responsible for all our hurt. But, at the moment, I need to be at my husband's side.'

'Why? Why, Laini, are these people so hell-bent on hurting you and Jax?'

That was the million-dollar question until all the information I have so far gathered together, like a Lego model. You have a bag of little Lego pieces. All you have to do is click them together to make a model of something.

I shrug my shoulders. I do not have time to get into this right now. Instead, I change the subject and say, *'Essy, I have to go back to my body every day or so, according to Betsy. If you're here, I say hello.'*

The steady beat of Jax's heart reminds me he is alive, and the medical machines beside his bed respond to each breath, each pump of his heart. His coloring over the last month or so has slowly improved.

Yesterday, well, I think it was yesterday. The doctor and nurse removed the tubing from the life-support machine from Jax. Thankfully, Jax continues to breathe unaided, and his heart remains strong.

His broken bones are healing nicely, along with his other internal injuries.

All the time I have stayed by his side, I have continued to speak to Jax. Letting him know I am here for him. I was convincing him to hang on. To fight. To keep living, not just for me, but also for himself.

With his nearly fatal injuries finally healing, the next step is to see if he will wake up.

'*Laini pet, you should be with your body. If you delay much longer, the connection between your spirit and your physical body will completely separate.*'

At the moment, I do not care about myself. How can I leave him? He is going to wake up. I just know it. I have to be here for when he does.

'*Betsy, at times, I wish to remain with Jax. If he had died, I would have stayed with him.*'

'*Laini pet, don't you ever speak like that again. You have two children to live for. Two!*'

'*Betsy, I know. It's just I could not bear to be separated from Jax again. Can you check on Jax's vitals? He is improving, right? So it's not just my imagination. Please tell me he is.*'

Betsy surveys my husband's body from her doctor's point of view. Reading each machine, he's still connected to and reviewing his charts. She nods and turns toward me. '*Laini pet. Your husband's vitals have improved. I wouldn't be surprised if he wakes soon.*'

That will be fantastic.

'*Are you sure, Betsy?*'

'*Positive, Laini pet. Now come on. You need to check in with your own body.*'

'*Okay. Let me say goodbye to Jax, and we'll leave.*'

*T*he lights emit a soft glow around the room my body is resting in. When I reach out and touch my physical body, a strange buzz flows through me, making me feel energized. This happens every time I touch my body.

'*Betsy, what have you noticed with my charts? Are the medical people my parents have hired...are they competent?*'

From her doctor's perspective. Betsy checks my chart, the medical machines, and my body.

'*As far as I can tell, your body has recovered from the emergency C-section. Your blood pressure is still low for being in a coma. Your other obs are what they should be. However, I cannot work out why you are not waking up?*'

'*Maybe I am waiting for Jax to arrive?*'

'*You never know, Laini pet, I have heard stranger things.*'

'*Betsy, have you visited my son?*'

'*No. I thought we should go to the nursery together. Come on, let's see your gorgeous boy.*'

Just as we approach the door to the nursery, a stranger in a nurse's uniform stops in front of the door and checks over their shoulder.

That is strange. I do not remember this person. '*Betsy, do you remember this nurse from our previous visits?*'

She shakes her head. '*No, Laini pet. There is*

something not quite right. Have you seen your mother or sister since we arrived?'

'No. I think I better find Essy.'

'Go. I'll keep watching over your boy.'

I concentrated on my sister and mist beside her as fast as I could. The second I glance around, I know she is not back in the apartment complex which belongs to our parents. Instead, she's down the street at the delicious bakery.

My sister releases a squeal before obtaining control of her vocal cords.

She smiles. *'Laini. Thank goodness you are okay. I have been worried sick. I haven't seen you in weeks.'*

'Essy, I came looking for you. I want to know who is the new nurse at our parents' apartment?'

She frowns and shakes her head. Before I can say anything else, Essy retrieves her cell from her back pocket and immediately phones someone.

"Hey, Mom. Do we have any new medical staff at the apartment?"

Essy glances at me and shakes her head.

'Where was this person when you saw them?'

'About to go into the nursery.'

"Um, mom. Can you check on Jacky? I think we have an intruder in his room." She shakes her head. I can see she is frustrated at whatever our mother is saying to her. "Code Red, mother. We have an intruder. Do not mess about. Go. I'll be there as fast as I can. Contact dad."

What are our parents doing? Why have they gone lax on security?

'Essy, why is the security at the penthouse failing?'

'I don't know, Laini, but we're going to find out.'

Essy races back to the apartment complex. She runs flat out, dodging people left and right until she reaches the front door.

The full-time security guard opens the door and welcomes her. His smile vanishes.

"Ms. Essy. What is it?"

"Code Red, McPower. Somehow, an intruder is in the building. Start the lockdown sequence. Is my father here?"

"No."

"Shut the elevators down until my father arrives and allow him access. And call in extra security. Now," she says over her shoulder as she races to the staircase.

Thank goodness she's still fit. It does not take her long to reach the penthouse apartment. She steps forward and has her eyes scanned in the security access point, unlocking the door.

We race down the hallway until our mother halts us at the side of the nursery doorway.

"Mom, what is happening?" Essy whispers.

With her gun in her hand, our mother stands rigid, staring into the nursery. I don't wait and mist past them straight into my baby's room.

Standing there with a pillow in one hand and a gun in the other is that nurse I had seen earlier.

'Laini pet. I tried to stop the bitch from smothering baby Jack with that pillow,' Betsy announces as she rushes to me. *'She just about peed when she heard me screech at her.'*

My focus is on my baby boy and watching his little chest. Oh, no. It fails to move. He should be taking in breaths. Something is not right.

'Essy, shoot the bitch. My son is not breathing,' I scream.

"Don't come near me, or I'll shoot the kid," the woman holding the gun demands.

'Essy, just shoot her. Shoot her now.'

'Just wait a second, Laini.'

'I said he is not breathing. My son does not have a second, Essy.' If only I could place my hands on him. *'He needs an ambulance.'*

'Hairy monkey balls. Okay, Laini.'

"Lady, move and put your gun down now," Essy barks.

With my focus on my son and keeping my back to the action behind me. I stop taking notice of what is happening. The next thing I hear is a loud gunshot. I turn to face the woman, only to find her body slumping to the floor.

"Essy. Why did you shoot her?" our mother demands.

"Are you serious right now, Mother?" My sister has her cell out and quickly speaks, requesting an ambulance as she rushes to the baby's crib. She glances back over her shoulder and says, "If you haven't noticed, little Jacky needs a hospital. That woman might have killed Jacky. How did she even get in here?" she says as her hand hovers over the baby's chest.

She frowns and picks him up. "Oh, geez. Look at his face. His lips are turning blue."

She instantly begins rubbing his back and front. He does not respond. She places him on his change table and listens for breaths. She shakes her head and then checks his mouth.

Essy then places her mouth over his mouth and nose, giving him a breath. She waits and then gives him another quick burst of air.

"Mother, call downstairs and inform them an ambulance is on its way," Essy says before giving little Jacky another breath. "Have security do a full sweep of the building."

She listens to his chest and mouth. Shakes her head and then gives Jacky another breath. "Come on, little man. Start breathing."

She places her ear on his chest. "Hairy monkey balls," she hisses.

She feels the middle of his chest. Then with two fingers, she begins chest compressions and starts counting under her breath. Once she reaches thirty or so, she gives Jacky two more breaths, then restarts chest compressions. She mumbles thirty and gives my boy two more breaths, then begins compressions once again. Once she says thirty, she pauses long enough, places her ear to his little chest, and listens.

'Essy, can you hear his heart beating?' I ask. She gives me a quick nod and gives Jacky another quick breath.

My little boy all at once kicks out with his legs. His chest expands as he drags in a breath before he releases a high-pitched cry.

Essy meets my eyes with tears in hers and a big smile as she brings Jack up against her chest.

"Thank goodness, Jack. You had us scared," she whispers beside his head, rubbing his back in comfort.

Noise from down the hall has me turning towards the open nursery door. My father appears with his gun in hand. His eyes dart around the room before landing on the baby.

"How's Jack?" he demands and uses his foot to move the weapon from the hand of the woman on the floor. "Who is she?"

He glances at my mother, then at Essy. She shrugs her shoulders and says, "I have no idea." And turns towards our mother.

Mother frowns and eyes the dead woman on the floor. "I don't recognize her. The nanny we hired should have been in here."

"I'd suggest you look for her," Essy murmurs, turns, and walks out of the nursery. The sound of the elevator dings to announce its arrival.

I mist to Essy in time to see two medics walk into the penthouse with equipment in their hands.

Once I knew my son was safe, I misted back to my husband, just in time to watch his eyes flutter several times before they open, revealing the hazel eyes I love so much.

Relief fills me.

'Thank goodness, Jax. You have had me so worried.'

His eyes meet mine. He frowns at me and then glances around him.

'Laini, where am I? Am I dead?'

I smile and shake my head. 'No, silly. You were taken and badly tortured. Rescued and brought here to this private hospital. Placed on life support, I've been waiting for you to wake.'

'Laini, why do you resemble a ghost?'

'Ahhh. That is a long story. Please, remember I am alive.'

'How can you be alive if you're here as a ghost?'

'Let's just concentrate on you.'

'How?'

'My love, I need you to recover. You must come to me.'

'What are you not telling me, Laini?'

'I better inform your doctor.'

'Laini, don't leave me.'

'Never, Jax. I have been here right by your side,' I murmur, as I mist to another room looking for the treating doctor.

*O*ver two weeks have passed, and Jax resembles more of his old self. The swelling around his eyes has all but gone. His broken bones have just about knitted together nicely. With his left leg still in a full plaster cast, he hobbles on his crutches to the bathroom.

What amazes me is that Jax has seen my ghostly form since the day he woke in the private hospital. And since then, he has requested that I remain in his room with him, fearing that he will not survive without me if I disappear. When I have time like this or while Jax sleeps, I would go back to my parents' penthouse to make contact with my body and check on my baby son and daughter. My hand hovers over my sleeping boy when I sense Betsy beside me. She stands there watching my baby.

'Laini, Jacky seems to come through unscathed after that dreadful woman smothering him with a pillow.'

My body flinches at her words. My boy could have died that day if it was not for Essy performing CPR.

I'm grateful to Essy for saving my baby boy.

I nod.

'We better head back to the hospital.' Speaking of... *'Um... Betsy, how is everything between you and Johnny?'*

Since remaining in this hospital with Jax, I've noticed Betsy come and go a lot. And when I see her with her estranged husband, their conversations are hushed.

'Laini pet, what do you think? I'm dead. My husband is alive. My daughter cannot see or hear me. And yes, I have gone to see her.'

'I'm sorry, Betsy. I didn't mean to sound inconsiderate.'

'No. I'm sorry, Laini pet. My life never turned out how I had dreamed.'

'Betsy, you died. So it kind of put an end to it.'

'Don't be a bitch, Laini. At least your body is still alive. Your daughter knows who you are and loves you.' Oh, crap. I felt like a bitch. Could Betsy be feeling sorry for herself or jealous of me?

We mist back to the hospital in time to see a stranger walking toward Jax's room. Who is he?

'Betsy, have you noticed that man before?'

She shakes her head. *'No. I think I better find Johnny. Go, and warn Jaxton.'*

I nod, don't wait for her to say anything else, and mist into my husband's room. Something is not right.

Chapter Twenty-Nine

LAINI

'm in mid-spin as I mist into my husband's private hospital room, instantly searching for Jax. My eyes focus on him using his crutches, hobbling through his bathroom door.

'Jax, an unknown man is heading this way.'

His head snaps in my direction, nearly causing him to stumble.

'Seriously. I'm not in the mood for visitors.'

'Sorry, babe. The man about to come in here does not look like a nice man. I'll say he's not a welcome visitor.'

'Shit. Can you alert anyone?'

'Betsy is searching for Johnny right now.'

Jax positions himself just inside the bathroom. Closing the door and snipping the little lock behind him.

The quiet creak of the hospital room door opening alerts us the man is entering the room.

'Laini, can you see what he is doing and let me know?'

'*Okay. Wait here,*' I say and mist beside the hospital bed.

The stranger is dressed in black sandshoes, denim jeans, and a shirt. Glances at the room. He reaches behind his back and pulls a handgun from beneath his shirt. Uh-oh.

'*Jax, block the door. The man has a gun,*' I call out.

'*Thanks. I'm using my crutch to block the door.*' Thank goodness.

I move and stand right in front of the stranger.

'*Who are you?*' I demand.

All the man in front of me does is look straight through me in his search for my husband. He even moved to the bed and lifted the bedding to check under it.

'*Jax, have you pushed the green emergency button beside the toilet?*'

'*What? No. You could have mentioned it earlier.*'

Within seconds, the sound of the bathroom alarm begins, quickly followed by rushed footsteps approaching the door. The man in front of me places his gun behind his back and moves towards the seat. Just as the door bursts open, the stranger sits down and smiles.

A nurse rushes in, quickly followed by a doctor. They both notice the stranger and frown, then go to the bathroom door.

"Mr. Travelli, are you okay in there?"

'*Come on, don't take your eyes off the stranger,*' I demand towards the staff.

As the seconds pass, the stranger slips out of the door undetected.

Uh-oh.

'Honey, that stranger has just left your room. You might as well open the door.'

'What do you mean, he has left? Left where?'

'How am I meant to know? Do you expect me to follow him?'

'It might be best if you do.' Thanks a lot, husband!

Well, color me in rainbows and tie my hair in ribbons. As usual it's up to a woman to handle the situation.

'Jax, somehow they've found you. Contact Essy with the cell Nigel gave you. Fill her in on what has happened. It's time you are moved to a new location.'

Before Jaxton replies, I mist and follow the stranger.

It does not take me long to discover where the gunman had disappeared to. I trail behind him as he runs along an alleyway. He turns a corner, and not far from the alley is a dark van idling on the main street. I mist inside and sit in the back as the stranger sits up front.

"Did yuh do it?" The female driver demands.

"No. He pushed de-emergency buddon in his washroom before I could reach him. His room soon filled with nurses." Thank goodness Jax pushed the nurse's call button.

"Grandfather will not be pleased." Too bad. Whomever grandfather is. No one is going to shoot my husband if I can help it.

He cringes and shrugs his shoulders. "Dat's a bad take."

The female driver drives off at a slow speed, most

likely not to bring any unwanted attention to them until she merges with other vehicles and pushes down on the accelerator.

Several minutes go by, maybe more. Their conversations only fill in some of the required information, I'm here to collect.

"Grandfather, I was prevented from shooting Travelli," the male stranger says into his cell.

Within seconds, he pulls the cell away from his head. Whomever Grandfather is, he is not happy and is now screaming at the stranger.

"Grandfather, we're on our way back. We'll try again." He shakes his head.

I then hear the other man's voice, "Susanna will be in contact later today." The stranger nods.

Huh? Who is Susanna? It must be a popular name. My mother's name is Susanna.

With enough courage, I concentrate on my sister and mist. When I open my eyes next, relief fills me — it worked. I'm at Essy's side.

'Laini. You need a bell. You'll give me a heart attack one of these days,' are her first words to me.

'Hello, to you too!' I dryly say.

'Oh, sorry. Hi, it's good to see you. Now. Jax contacted me. Was there an armed man in his hospital room? What is happening?'

I nod and reply, *'I followed the stranger. He left in a dark van with a woman driver, and they were heading north.'* Essy opens an app on her cell and quickly adds the information I had gathered, including the vehicle's registration plate, the phone conversation, and the address of the private hospital.

Once she has all the information, Essy begins making her phone calls. Hearing her organize for Jax to be moved to our parents' private apartment fills me with mixed emotions. Will it be safe? Will more trouble follow?

The nagging feeling about this Grandfather person… My gut is warning me about something. It's just a question of what it is. *'I wonder who this grandfather character is?'*

'Yes, we need to discover who he is and if he has something to do with the mafia?'

'You think he might?' My gut feeling increases.

'Laini, you never know. As for this other woman named Susanna… I wonder who she is. Can you gather more information about her?'

'I'll try. And Essy, please protect my husband. I feel something is wrong, and it's heading our way.'

With a cheeky smile, she replies, *'I'll try.'*

LAINI

Concentrating on the stranger, I mist right by his side.

Wow. I'm getting good at this. Moving freely, transporting in a blink of an eye. An important part I must remember is that if I don't become one with my body soon, I might remain like this forever, and I'll never be able to touch my husband or kids again physically.

The other part I soon discover is misting into someone's bathroom while they take a leak, is not a pleasant sight. Gross, really. As I float in the bathroom to witness firsthand that they do not wash their hands properly... disturbing.

The stranger steps out of the bathroom and walks down a long corridor. If I'm not mistaken, I swear we are in some old-style mansion. Where are we?

Just up from us, an older version of the stranger appears. This new man is wearing a dark blue suit and not black jeans like the guy I've been following.

Maybe we are now in a family home. With any luck, I'll discover who this grandfather is, as well as the other information we are seeking. "Paulie, hurry. Grandfather wants to see you."

"I'm coming. Geez, I had to go to de-washroom, paps." Anyone listening to the stranger would know he is from Chicago from his slang Chicago speech alone. Thank goodness my speech improved when I moved away from Chicago all those years ago.

"You have let us down, Paulie. You will be lucky to take on another assignment for grandfather."

"Paps, it's hard to shoot someone when de-small room fills with witnesses."

"That is no excuse, my boy. Grandfather will most likely punish you."

"Seriously, Paps?"

"Grandfather wanted Travelli dead. Chances he will be moved. No worries. We can still get to him if he is moved. We are just waiting for your aunt. She'll let us know what is happening."

Aunt? Who is this aunt?

"Paps, how'd Aunt Susanna remain undercover for all de-hese years? I thought Grandfather would have killed her for her failings years ago."

"You stupid boy. Your aunt has remained our primary source of information all these years. If it weren't for her, we would have been caught years ago, and you would not be here now."

My thoughts race, attempting to think who this Susanna woman is, and undercover where? What has she done for this Paulie character wanting her dead?

I continue following the two men into another room containing hundreds, if not thousands, of books. Wow! This library would give my parents' state-of-the-art library a run for its money.

The man known as Paps steps toward the bookshelf on our right and selects a red cover book on the second shelf from the bottom. Instead of removing the book from the shelf, he pulls it at an angle. A click follows, and part of the bookshelf moves forward, revealing a doorway.

Paulie follows Paps through the opening into a dimly lit wide passageway with narrow red strip lighting along the floor's edge.

"Paps, when will Grandfather improve de-lighting around here?"

"Paulie, stop your whining. Remember to keep your mouth shut and only speak when asked."

"Paps, come now. Grandfather will do nothing to me. He loves me. I'm his favorite grandson."

"My son. I hope you are right. Remember, stop using the Chicago slang when speaking to Grandfather. It will only irritate him."

The man in the suit, now known as Paps, otherwise Chicago slang for Pops, knocks on a solid oak door. My attention focuses on a small speaker left of the door where a deep male voice sounds. "Philip, good of you to arrive so promptly. Bring Paulie in. We have much to discuss."

"Shit, this is not good," I hear Pops murmur under his breath. At least now I've learned Pops' real name is Philip.

Philip opens the door. Both men walk in. I move forward and freeze. The vision in front of me... I think I blinked several times. The elderly man — I know him. Right in front of me is a man from my past. A friend of my murdered parents — the one who is said to have killed my parents. That man is in charge of the Apolo syndicate. Uncle Pedro.

"Father, as you can see, Paulie is here to discuss what happened today."

The steely eyes of Pedro Apolo harden at Paulie.

Pedro remains in his seat and stares. Paulie stumbles and quickly rights himself.

Pedro's lips twitch, and then he sneers. "You, boy, are a disgrace to the Apolo name. How can you fail an easy target?"

Paulie hangs his head. "I am sorry, Grandfather. Before I could shoot him, de-room filled with nurses."

"That is no excuse," Pedro yells. Paulie's head snaps up, and his legs shake. "Boy, come here."

Paulie glances at his father. But Philip keeps staring straight ahead. Paulie gulps, steps forward and stops at the edge of the large timber desk.

"Place your hand down on the table, Paulie."

Paulie glances at his father again, but his father keeps staring ahead.

Very slowly, Paulie places his shaking hand down flat on the desk. Then, before I could blink, Pedro slams a medium serrated knife down on Paulie's pinky finger, removing the tip. Blood pools, and all Paulie does is stare at his hand. Philip quickly grabs his son's hand and wraps a hanky around the fingers.

"Now, when you are given an order, obey it. And remember, stop speaking as gutter filth from Chicago. Practice your English. Now get out of here."

"Yes, Grandfather," Paulie croaks, turns and exits the room.

"Was that necessary, Father?"

"You know it was, Philip. Now go. Make sure the idiot does not bleed all over my house."

"Yes, Father." Philip bows his head, turns and exits the room.

Not sure what to do, I stare at the man who used to bounce me on his knee and make me laugh.

He is no man. He's a monster.

Pedro opens a side drawer, removes a pack of cleaning wipes, and slowly removes the spilled blood and the tip of Paulie's finger from his desk, throwing the soiled wipes into his trash can by his feet.

His cell phone pings with an incoming video call as he sits up in his oversized leather office chair.

He swipes the screen and smiles. "Hello, my dear. How is everything going at your end?"

A chill races up my spine when I hear the other person's voice.

"Hello, Papa. I noticed Paulie failed. Never mind, Jaxton is on his way here. My daughter, Essy, will deliver him straight into my hands."

Now, I felt frozen. My mother is speaking to Pedro.

I'm confused.

What in the hell is going on?

Before I knew what to do, I began screaming for

Betsy, *'Betsy.'* I need Betsy. She'll know what to do. *'Betsy. I need you. I need you here, now!'*

The familiar sensation I have felt since I was a young teenager spreads through my body. I glance to my right, and there she is, in all her glory, with a frown.

'What is it, Laini pet? Why are you in this man's office?'

'Why?' I shake my head, trying to get my brain to function. *'I followed the man who attempted to shoot Jax today. His name is Paulie. He came straight here.'*

Before I can complete my sentence, Betsy announces, *'This Paulie fellow spoke to this man?'* All I can do is nod. *'Do you remember this man, Laini pet?'*

My focus remains on the man. I nod again. *'Yes.'*

'He is the one who wanted me dead and succeeded.' She kept looking between Pedro and me before saying, *'Why am I here, Laini pet? I never wanted to see this man ever again.'*

I nod and mouth, *sorry*. Then, with a flick of my head towards the killer, I say, *'Betsy, look at who he is speaking with on his cell.'*

Betsy frowns again but does not hesitate. She moves behind the dangerous man, and her eyes just about bulged out of her ghostly head. Her eyes meet mine. *'No, there must be some mistake.'*

I shake my head. *'No. I wish I were.'*

We pause long enough to listen to more of Pedro and my mother's conversation.

"What are you going to do regarding Essy and Laini?"

"I don't know. Laini is as good as dead." What the

world... Geez, thanks a lot, mother, for all the love. "As for Essy, we have to tread carefully. She is far too much like her father. She is too good at her job."

"If she cannot be brought over to our side, you know you have to kill her, don't you?"

What the? Is this man serious? Surely Mother would never go down that path.

"Papa, the baby brat, should have died, but Essy came in and saved the child. I do not want any child from Jaxton Travelli under my roof."

What? How dare she say that? Anger fills me.

"Your daughter was smart not to reveal the father of her baby girl."

"If I had known, I would have made her terminate the pregnancy."

Say what? How can she say such a thing!

"Don't forget. Jaxton Travelli has links to an interstate mafia family." Hang on. What is Pedro speaking about? "They're enemies. Never doubt that. The result was not good for us when the boy married his ex-wife with two interstate mafia families merging as one. It could have been our downfall. His refusal to assist the families with his FBI contacts was our blessing. But now, that boy has opened too many cans of worms. He must die."

"I agree."

I don't think so.

Over my comatose body.

Chapter Thirty-One

LAINI

'*Betsy, my life has just imploded. We have to warn Essy.*'

'*I agree. You go and speak with Essy. I'll remain here and gather more information.*'

I nod. How much more do we want to know? I then concentrate on Essy and mist.

My world has fallen on its axis. Right, this minute, I think of my biological mother. It goes to show we never knew her. She's been undercover all this time. Oh, my poor father. I wonder if he ever suspected?

Essy is with my husband, speaking to him in my old bedroom in my parents' penthouse apartment.

What in the world am I going to do? We have to get Jax out of here. I grab her attention and tilt my head toward the door. She nods in understanding.

"Jax, I'll be back in a minute. Gotta go to my old room to grab something."

"Okay. I'll be right here," he sarcastically says.

As soon as she steps out of my old bedroom, she

heads to her old bedroom, straight to the ensuite, and turns the tap on.

'*Laini. You're finally back,*' Essy says, a little snippy.

I shake my head. '*Sis, remember I love you.*'

Essy frowns. '*What has happened?*'

'*Essy, I need you to move Jax to somewhere safe with our children.*'

'*Laini, what are you talking about?*'

'*Trust me on what I am about to reveal.*'

She nods. Her face changes to her old FBI persona. '*What did you learn?*'

'*If I said our mother has been working fully undercover since before she married Dad, what would you say?*'

'*As I said. What did you learn? And what do you mean, our mother has been undercover?*'

'*Just that. Our darling mother is part of the Apolo Syndicate.*'

Essy shakes her head in disbelief. '*Huh. How? I didn't see that one coming.*'

'*Yeah. Not what I wanted to discover listening to our mother speaking with Pedro Apolo. Otherwise known as Uncle Pedro to me. Grandfather to his family. Or to our mother, Papa.*'

'*Oh, my hairy monkey balls.*'

'*You can say that again. Our so-called long-lost family wants Jax dead. If they had known Emma was Jax's daughter, mother would have had me terminate the pregnancy when I was seventeen.*'

'*Holy shit. Seriously.*'

I nod. '*What is our next step?*'

'Thankfully, I had arranged for the children to go to the park.' Essy pauses. I can see the moment she comes up with an idea. *'We'll all go into hiding. Our parents do not know everything about us.'*

I nod and reply, *'Thank goodness for that.'*

'I'll have Dekk's jet on standby. The only thing I don't know is our destination.'

I nod. As long as we can get away from here and everyone is safe. *'Essy, Pedro Apolo, and mother said Jax is from a mafia family. So had his ex-wife.'*

'Oh, my. This day just keeps getting better.'

My sister shakes her head, pulls her cell from her pocket, and makes the necessary phone calls. The first one was to one of her employee bodyguards, who is acting as a nanny for our kids.

"Hello, Jasmine. Code pineapple. This is not a drill. You are required to keep the kids away from the apartment complex." She nods several times. Thank goodness our kids are not here. Since the fake nurse episode, Essy had her people watch the kids. "Listen, tell the kids they can have a special treat from the bakery and pick out something for the adults to eat for dessert." The kids will love that. "...Yes, call in your backup. ...I'll be in touch. Be prepared to fly out of here."

I grab Essy's attention. *'Is Jack with them?'* I demand. She nods and smiles at me. That is a relief. All the kids are safe for now.

Just as I go to turn, the familiar buzz begins just before Betsy appears.

'Laini pet, we have a problem.'

Chapter Thirty-Two

LAINI

'What kind of problem?' I demand.

'Your mother. She's got her gun and heading this way.'

'She's what? No. We have to stop her.'

I turn back to Essy as she ends her call. *Essy, we gotta go. Grab your gun. Mother is on her way to take Jax out.*

'Oh, shit. I'll never forgive mother for treating us like her personal pawns in this homicidal game. Who would do that to her own children?'

'Don't know, but she is turning out to be one twisted bitch.'

Essy flushes her toilet, turns the tap off and grabs her bag from her closet, and pulls out one of her handguns. She checks the clip and places the gun at her back, making sure her jacket covers the butt, then carefully maneuvers her way down the hall toward my room.

'Laini pet. Nigel and Johnny are here. How are we to let them in?'

'I'll show you. Come on.' We mist to where the two men are waiting. With an old digital lock at the back entrance, I explain what the codes are. Nigel mentioned he had contacted my father. From the way Nigel is speaking, I think they knew about mothers' past.

Great!

Thanks for giving us the heads up.

It doesn't take Nigel and Johnny long to enter the penthouse apartment. I mist to Essy. I need to know if I have missed anything.

"Essy, why don't you go down the street to the bakery and grab a box of pastries for afternoon tea? I bet the kids would love them." Now that is interesting. Our mother must not know the children are out of the building.

"Momma, not right now. I'm waiting for Jax to come out of the bathroom. Then, I'll be questioning him about what has happened."

"I can do that. Or we can wait together."

Essy shakes her head. "Mother, why did you become an FBI agent?"

"Why the questions, Essy?"

"One of my boys was asking me why I became an FBI agent, and he also wanted to know why you and Daddy had become an agent as well."

"Well, when my grandson is a little older, I might just tell him. But not today."

"Momma, are you feeling okay? You look pale.

Maybe you should go lie down for a little while. I'll contact Daddy to bring home pizza for everyone."

If mother fell for that, I'd be amazed. The foul woman is determined to kill my husband.

"Essy, I am feeling perfectly fine. Unfortunately, your father is not due to be home until late tonight. He has been kept back at FBI headquarters."

"Really? Is everything okay?"

"It is none of your concern. You no longer work there, so butt out."

Wow. Touchy! Mother is becoming annoyed.

Just then, a sound comes from the kitchen. I know full well it should be Nigel and Johnny.

"Who is that? No one should be in the kitchen."

"What are you talking about, Mother? Surely one of the kids is grabbing a drink? Don't be so paranoid."

"I'll see who is in the kitchen. I'll be back in a minute."

Essy glances at me. *'Get Jax out of here.'*

'How. She'll see him. We have to do something.'

The next thing we hear is mother's loud voice, "What are you doing in my home, Nigel?"

"Move, Susanna. Put your weapon down and sit down at the kitchen table."

"Get that gun off me, you silly fool. I have orders."

"No, Susanna. Your days are finished. Pedro has given me orders to shoot you."

"What? No. He just gave me orders" Mother stops talking when she realizes she has said too much.

"What did Pedro Apolo want you to do?"

"Nothing. I meant."

Before Nigel can blink, Mother pulls her second gun out and shoots Nigel in the head. He slumps to the floor.

Essy appears with her gun aimed at our Mother. "What is going on? Who was shot?"

Mother lifts her gun higher at Essy. "Daughter, you do not understand what is going on. Nigel here was going to shoot me."

Essy takes several steps to the side. First, she glances at Nigel, then at Mother. "Why, Mother? Why did you do it?"

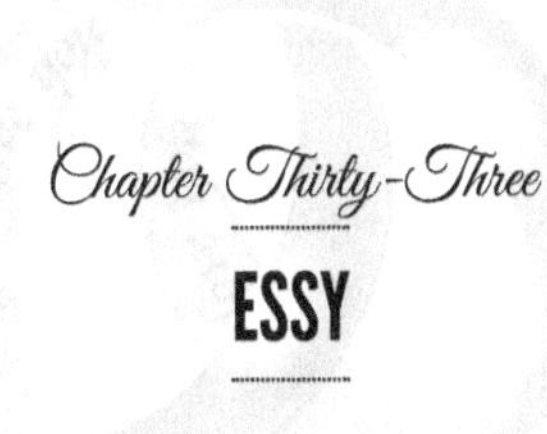

Chapter Thirty-Three

ESSY

'*Laini, get Jax out of here.*' I demand while keeping my focus on our mother.

'*Don't do anything stupid,*' Laini says. '*We both know this will not end well.*' After those words, she then disappears from the corner of my eye.

With my gun trained on my mother, I know I must tread carefully until help arrives. She doesn't answer my question. Instead, she tilts her head to the side as if she is contemplating something.

Alrighty, then. It looks like I'll have to use my acting skills to get out of this one. I have to have faith she still loves me enough to lower her gun.

My mother smiles at me, and I smile back and say, "Mother, thank goodness you shot Nigel." Mother gives me a strange look. Glances at the body on the ground, then back to me. "When I recently discovered he's been working with the mafia. My heart broke. How could the man do that to us? He was my uncle! Our friend."

Mother lowers her weapon. "It goes to show you truly do not know anyone in this world."

I shake my head — words from the woman who has lied to me my whole life. "I never knew the man could become so heartless. I wonder if he was here to finish off Laini?" Shit, I should not have said that. Now, Mother is going to start thinking back to her order to kill Jax. Then maybe Laini and me. "I think we better call the police and have Nigel removed before the kids see."

Mother shakes her head and says, "Essy, see to the children and ensure they stay in the games room. I'll phone the police."

"Okay."

I turn my back on my mother, hoping she does not shoot me. As I walk down the hallway, I glance over my shoulder and notice mother walking toward Laini's bedroom.

Oh, hairy monkey balls. I turn back around and follow her. I have to warn Laini.

Chapter Thirty-Four

LAINI

*E*ssy keeps Mother talking, as I mist to Jax.

'*Hey, baby. How are you going?*' my gorgeous husband says.

'*Jax, did you hear the gunshot?*'

Jax glances around and stands carefully, placing his crutches in place to keep him up.

'*I thought it was one of the kids. What is going on, Laini?*'

'*Jax, I need you to get out of this building. My mother is planning on shooting you.*'

He frowns. '*Me? Why?*'

'*Honey, we do not have time. We have to go.*'

He nods and slowly makes his way out of the door. '*Which way?*'

'*Towards the elevator. Mother is in the kitchen.*'

Jax hobbles his way down the hallway, avoiding the kitchen end of the apartment. Just as he reaches the elevator, I hear Essy in my head.

'*Laini, watch out. Mother is coming.*'

Shit.

Jax leans forwards and pushes the down arrow. Somehow, I don't think the elevator will arrive in time.

'Laini, too late. Mother knows Jax is not in your room.'

Uh-oh.

I scream for *Betsy*.

I just hope she can help.

The familiar sensation announcing Betsy surrounds me, and I turn in time to see her appear.

She quickly glances about. *'Laini pet, I have Johnny sneaking into our location. I hope he can help.'*

Just as the elevator pings, my mother appears.

Uh-oh. We're out of time.

"Where do you think you're going, Jaxton? Shouldn't you be lying down or resting with your leg up?"

"Ah, Susanna. I was on my way to the roof for some fresh air."

Before Jax says another word, mother lifts her gun and points it at my husband. No... No, don't shoot him.

"Now, Jax. You are going to make your way back to the kitchen. We'll have a nice little chat."

I glance over mother's shoulder and see Essy appear.

"Mother, did you call the police yet? I'll call downstairs and tell them the police will be here shortly."

Just as Mother turns towards Essy, Johnny steps from another room straight in front of Jax. Pushing him back into the open elevator.

"Hello, Little Sussie. It has been a long time,"

Johnny announces, causing mother to twist at the sound of his voice.

"What in the world? Is that truly you, Johnny Blue?" she smiles.

"It is. Now, why don't you put your gun down?" Her smile vanishes before she sneers at him.

"No. I don't think so. Why are you here?"

Johnny smiles. "I have my orders, Little Sussie. You have yourself in a bit of a pickle."

"Did Papa send you?" she queries before frowning.

"It seems you have been a naughty girl. And as usual, I have to clean up after you."

"What are you speaking about? Who gave you the orders?" she demands.

He paused long enough to make it look as if he was thinking about something. "Did you ever discover why you miscarried that child all those years ago, Little Sussie?"

"What has that got to do with anything? Why are you asking me that now, after all these years?"

"No reason, really. I had wondered if Papa had explained why he did it."

Mother frowns at Johnny. "What are you talking about? What did Papa do?"

Johnny chuckles before making his face turn serious. "Little Sussie. Papa never wanted his adopted prize to produce children, not of his choosing, anyway."

"What? Who's adopted? I don't understand?"

"He never told you, did he?"

"Tell me what?"

"Why, Little Sussie. You are, of course. One of his

mistresses had a child. It turns out you were not his. He wasn't happy to learn his gorgeous little daughter was not his child after all. So, he had the mother killed. His plan all along was to use you. His own little secret weapon. And what a weapon you have been."

"No." Mother shakes her head. "I don't believe you."

Well, if my mother is not blood-related to the mafia boss, Pedro Apolo, I am incredibly relieved. Who wants to be related to that animal? I glance at Essy. She nods. I can see she, too, is pleased to learn this bit of information.

"Did you know, Pedro, had my wife and child killed?"

Mother frowns and shakes her head. "No. You were never married."

"Says Pedro. Yet, I was married. We had a child on the way. Whose house do you think he claimed? Your daughter had lived in the same house years later until it was destroyed. That house had belonged to my wife."

"What...no. No one knows of Laini's real identity."

"Are you fooling yourself, Sussie? Pedro has known several years now."

"No!"

"If she hadn't married her husband, her identity would have remained unknown."

"I don't understand?"

"Pedro only had known Laini as one of your long-lost embryos. He hadn't known she was, in fact, the daughter of Keith and Dorothy Lewis. That is another reason dear old papa wanted her dead."

"No," Mother shakes her head.

Johnny lifts his gun. "Time to end this, Susanna. It all stops today."

Mother lifts her gun and aims it at Johnny's chest. "No. Johnny. You're the only one who will be stopped today. I am Papa's favorite."

Johnny chuckles. "Stop fooling yourself, Sussie. Pedro has men on their way here to ensure you and your family never see another sunset."

I glance at Essy. She has remained quiet throughout the conversation. I hope she has a backup planned because we'll need it.

Mother's voice brings my focus back to her. "No. Papa will never terminate me."

"You silly little fool. You were only a means to an end."

Essy's cell dings, alerting her to an incoming message.

Mother spins and points her gun at Essy.

"Whoa. Mom. It's only me. I have a text from my husband." Mother shakes her head. I can see she is confused, which is not a good sign. "Momma. Put your gun down."

Mother's head snaps back up and glares at Essy. "What do you know of Pedro Apolo?"

Essy shakes her head. "Not much. Apart from he's the boss of the Apolo Syndicate. Why? Is what this stranger...Johnny, say is true? Are you Pedro Apolo's daughter?"

"Adopted," Johnny says.

Mother spins and aims her gun at Johnny's head. "No. I am his daughter. I am not adopted!"

Too many things happen at once.

I hear Betsy scream to Johnny for him to shoot Susanna. The sound of two gun blasts fills our ears.

My mother looked stunned before falling to the ground, followed by Johnny with a bleeding bullet wound to his forehead.

Betsy screams, and her ghostly form goes to her beloved.

Essy moves and kicks the gun away from our mother's hand, then leans down to check for a pulse. She glances at me and shakes her head. She then swipes the screen of her cell and lifts it to her ear.

"Daddy, we have a situation. Johnny and Nigel are both dead. Mother shot them both." She nods, then shakes her head. "No, Dad...Mother is dead." She nods her head to whatever our father is saying. "Yes, we require a clean-up crew..." She nods again. "...Yes, that will require my IT guys." She then mumbles a few more words and then ends the call.

She steps to the elevator with its door wide open. Oh, god. My husband. In all the horrifying excitement, I forgot about my husband. I move beside Essy and look in. My husband is leaning against the wall, protected by the little panel.

"Come on out, Jax. You better go and wait in the room where Laini's body is."

He nods and begins his awkward movements past the two dead bodies. He pauses and shakes his head, glancing from Johnny to my mother. Then continues down the hall with Essy at his side.

Chapter Thirty-Five

LAINI

watch my husband hobble toward the room where my body is kept. One thought had crossed my mind. Where is the nurse who takes care of my body? Or had my mother planned on killing us all?

I shake my head and go beside Betsy. The poor woman is blubbering over her husband. If she could physically cry, she would have a flood of tears streaming down her face.

A light begins to glow in front of us, and as I watch, a ghostly form materializes into a spirit shape of Johnny as he sits up from his body and glances towards Betsy.

'Betsy. What is it, my love?'

Betsy pauses and looks up at his ghostly form. 'Johnny, that bitch shot you. I am so sorry, my love.'

Johnny glances around the foyer. To the body of my mother. Then down at his own body.

'Oh, shit. No. No, no, no. I can't be dead!'

'I am so sorry, Johnny.'

A movement to my right has me turning my head. There, floating above her body is my mother. Our eyes meet. *'Laini. What are you doing here? What is going on?'* she demands.

'Mother, you're dead. That is what is happening.'

'What? No. That cannot be right.'

'Believe it, Susanna. You're dead.'

'But...but.'

'No buts. Just dead.'

'What about you... are you dead too? Did that nurse kill you?'

Nurse? Oh, boy. That does not sound good.

I scream out for Essy. *'Essy, shoot the nurse.'*

The next thing I hear is a gunshot. *'Essy, are you okay?'*

'Yes, don't worry about Jax or myself. The nurse was injecting you with something. Sorry, I just ripped your intravenous line from your hand.'

'You what?'

'She had a gun pointing at us and a vial of something I have not seen before. It looked dangerous.'

I glance at my mother. *'Was the nurse here to kill me if things went south?'*

Sadly, my mother nods. *'I'm so sorry, Laini. I never wanted Pedro to get his hands on you and be manipulated. And trust me. He would have.'* Too much has happened for me to believe her.

'Does Daddy know? Does he know you were working undercover for the mafia?'

She shakes her head. *'No. I fell in love with him. He was only meant to be my cover while working in the FBI.'*

'*Can I believe you right now? Did you even love Essy and me?*'

'*Yes. I do with all my heart. But, Laini, there is something you need to know. Both you and Essy have a brother out there. There was another embryo. I kept his identity from your father and Pedro. I wanted him to be safe. He is in the Marines. I am so proud of him. I know he is retiring soon, and I emailed Essy his resume to become a bodyguard.*'

Huh. Essy and I have a brother? How is that possible? '*What is his name?*'

'*His name is Tarret James Browns.*'

My mind is ready to explode. Why didn't she ever tell us? '*Are you serious right now? Where has he been all this time? How did you find him?*' I demand.

'*A month or so after I lost my baby, I ran into a couple I had recognized from the same fertility clinic. They said they were pregnant. I told them to leave for their safety and not to tell anyone how they became pregnant. Since then, I have kept in contact with them through the years. I had the baby's DNA tested. The test was conclusive. He was mine. So, I ensured he got into the right schools and had the best chances in life.*'

Essy walks back down the hallway and stands there shaking her head. She heard every word.

"I had seen his resume and EOI form on my desk this week with several others. I haven't had time to process the new interview candidates." Essy looks from me and back to our mother. "You should have told us, Susanna. Does this Tarret know we are his family?"

Susanna shakes her head. *'No. He only knows me as his godmother.'*

Oh, geez.

"Tell me where all the information you have on him and any other information we need to know."

Susanna nods and speaks with Essy. I turn and face Betsy and Johnny. If I could, I would have tears in my eyes, for they were holding one another — something they haven't done in decades.

'Um, guys. What is next?'

Betsy turns and smiles at me. *'Laini pet, I am going to show Johnny what life as a spirit is all about. Oh, I will be back. I need to discuss a few things with you. Please take care.'*

I nod and watch both Betsy and Johnny mist away before my eyes. I wonder where they are going. Maybe to check on their daughter?

Essy moves closer and checks our mother's pockets. She removes a set of keys and her necklace, sliding them into her pocket.

The elevator dings. Within seconds the doors open, and our father walks into the foyer with several of his trusted staff, Davies, Jones, and Beatty.

"Holy shit. Susanna is dead." Our father went down on his knees beside his dead wife.

'James. James, can you hear me?' Susanna screams. Our father doesn't respond to her. Instead, she turns and looks at both Essy and me. *'Why can't he hear me?'*

I wasn't going to say or give her an answer. I just shake my head. As for Essy, she replies, *'I don't know,*

Susanna. Laini and I have always been different. What do you want Father to know? I will inform him.'

I've had enough of my so-called mother. Instead of staying around, I mist to the room where my body is kept.

Chapter Thirty-Six

LAINI

The first thing I see when I mist into the room is my husband holding my physical hand. He looks so lost. If only I knew how to get my spirit form back into my solid body. Thankfully, I do not see the fake nurse. Essy must have moved her.

'Jax, are you okay?'

My husband looks up and meets my eyes, and smiles. *'Hey, baby. Do you have any idea how to get back into your body?'*

I shake my head. *'No.'*

Jax releases my physical hand and sits back in his chair. *'How's everything going out there?'*

'My father has just arrived. He's not able to see my mother's ghost, and she keeps calling out to him.'

'Oh, my. Does that mean I am special, that I can see and hear you?'

I move and hover, straddling his legs just like I used to when I was a full-bodied person. *'Yes. You're my special man.'* My ghostly hands hover over his face. All I can do is lean my ghostly head nearly against his head. *'I love you, Jax.'*

'I love you, Laini.'

We remain in that position, a position we have repeated many times before through the years. We soak one another in, enjoying the moment until Essy walks into the room several minutes or maybe hours later.

Our heads snap towards Essy. The first thing I notice is something in her hands.

"Guys, Dad is going to call the police." I move from Jax's lap and hover by Essy to look closer at her hands. "We don't have much time." Does she have candles? Why would she need candles? "I also had an interesting call from Brayd."

Huh? What has Brayd got to do with anything?

"Brayd?" My husband's voice has me turning toward him. "Whose Brayd?" Jaxton asks, glancing back and forth between Essy and me. Now, this is going to be awkward.

"Brayd used to date, Laini. Jax, before you say anything. They ended things on good terms as they discovered they were better off as friends."

Jax looks at me and gives me his look with a raised eyebrow. I burst out giggling at his antics. *'Yes, Jax. Brayd and I are friends. Since I've been in this ghostly spirit form, I do not have full memories of the time I was with him.'*

Jax shakes his head and turns to Essy. "As you were saying. What was the interesting conversation?"

Essy eyes me and motions for me to move closer to

her. "Laini, Brayd has made many inquiries... Regarding your predicament."

'Has he discovered how I am to merge my ghostly spirit form with my physical body?'

Essy's face lights up with a full-bloom smile. "Yes. Yes, he does."

Excitement fills me. *'Don't just stand there, sister, out with it. What do I have to do?'*

Essy's smile turns into her serious face. She then turns to Jax.

"Jaxton, I need you to stand beside Laini's body." She turns to me and says, "Now, Laini, I need you to hover above your body. Lay flat."

Okay. I can do that.

I do as Essy says and hover horizontally flat, barely above my still physical body.

"Jax, with your hands' palms facing down over the spiritual form of Laini and repeat after me."

Jax nods and hovers his hands over me. He looks straight at me and smiles. "You ready, Laini? I cannot wait to hold you in my arms again. Remember, I love you."

I nod. *'I love you, Jaxton Travelli, with my whole body and soul.'*

"Yeah, yeah. Come on, guys. Time is ticking," Essy deadpans, placing the last of the candles she brought with her strategically around my body and lighting each one. "It is recommended to add candles to this little ceremony."

Jax and I shrug, then smile at one another before turning our heads to look at Essy.

If candles are required, then light away! Essy hasn't said not to, but I'm going to recite the words she says. Everything little thing might help.

"Right. Now that we are all ready, let's begin," she declares as she moves to the other side of the bed and places her outstretched hands above me. "Repeat after me. 'One of thee.'"

I repeat with Jax, "One of thee."

"Spirit of soul, return to thee."

Jax raises his brow, and we repeat, "Spirit of soul, return to thee."

"Body of soul, open for thee spirit," Essy chants.

"Body of soul, open for thee spirit," Jax and I repeat.

"Body and soul join together to become one."

"Body and soul join together to become one," Jax and I copy.

"Blessed mother and all there is, allow Laini to become one. Join her spirit and body thee to become one. Blessed be."

We repeat. "Blessed mother and all there is, allow Laini to become one. Join her spirit and body thee to become one. Blessed be."

"May our words ring true and allow Laini guidance back to her physical body. May the love of the Goddess be forever in our hearts and never tear Laini apart. Merry meet. And, merry part. And merry meet again. Body and soul join together to become one. Now Laini will be one. Blessed be." Wow. Now that is a big mouthful. Am I going to remember all the words?

Jax looks at Essy with both eyebrows raised, shakes his head, and repeats, "May our words ring true and allow Laini guidance back to her physical body. May the love of the Goddess be forever in our hearts and never tear Laini apart. Merry meet. And, merry part. And merry meet again. Body and soul join together to become one. Now Laini will be one. Blessed be."

Jax looks down at me and mouths, *'I love you.'* Then glances back at Essy.

"Now with me, and remember to concentrate and repeat each verse simultaneously. Keep chanting until Laini's ghostly spirit has returned inside her body."

Jax nods. He takes a deep breath, then releases.

As one, we begin.

"One of thee,
Spirit of soul, return to thee,
Body of soul, open for thee spirit
Body and soul join together to become one.
Blessed mother and all there is, allow Laini to
    become one.
Blessed be.
May our words ring true, allow Laini guidance
    back to her physical body.
May the love of the Goddess be forever in our
    hearts and never tear Laini apart.
Merry meet.
And, merry part.
And merry meet again.
Body and soul join together to become one.
Now Laini will be one.
Blessed be."

They kept on repeating every word, every verse, faster and faster until I felt my ghostly spirit being pulled down into my physical body. A sensation of pins and needles fills me until they explode throughout my form. My spirit form and physical body wavered until they settled into one — two halves fusing back together to become one in body and soul. Relief fills me. Before I have the chance to look at Jax, everything turns black.

Chapter Thirty-Seven

ESSY

*O*h, my hair, monkey balls. I think we've done it. Laini's ghostly spirit has vanished inside her body. There was a shimmer of bright light followed by calmness.

Well, I think we've done it. I bloody hope we have.

I finish the last line with Jax.

"Now, Laini, be one. Blessed be."

We pause and glance at one another, then look down at Laini.

Laini's coloring is better. The medical machines indicate her blood pressure is now at a normal level, and her heart rate is beating at a normal speed instead of the slow beats I had been used to hearing.

"Do you think we did it?" Jax quietly asks.

"I hope so. Look, sit back down with her. I have to speak with my dad. I have a lot to discuss with him before the police arrive."

"Okay. I have to sit anyway. Essy, I want to thank you for all you have done."

"You're welcome, Jax. I better remove these candles then go."

With the smoldering candles in my hand, I walk back along the hallway until I reach the lounge area, where my father sits with two of my team IT members on the lounge chairs. They seem to be in serious discussions. I turn and head to the foyer, where my mother and Johnny's body are covered with a blanket. I glance around but do not see my mother's ghostly form anywhere. I don't even see that bright light, either. I have to speak to Dad regarding Mom. How much does he really know?

As I approach my dad, he looks up and gives me a sad smile. "Dad, how are you going?" I ask. He shakes his head.

"Numb, Essy. Numb."

Poor Daddy. I nod. It's understandable. They had been a couple for a long time.

"Have the police been called?"

He shakes his head. "No. Not yet. First, we must set everything up. When we phone, we'll call for an ambulance first, then the police." Thank goodness. I have much to discuss with Dad. Dad turns to me. "You mentioned the nurse was injecting Laini when you shot her."

I nod. "Yes. If I hadn't shot her and removed Laini's intravenous line, she might be dead now."

Dad shakes his head again. "Essy, the police are going to be asking a lot of questions. I don't know where to start." First, we are going to require a good cover story.

"Dad, I discovered mother has been undercover for the mafia all these years. Her father, Pedro Apolo, had sent her to learn and become an FBI agent. He only did it because he was using her. He discovered she was not his biological daughter and had Susanna's mother killed for her deception. There is a lot we need to discuss. Look, Johnny Apolo and Uncle Nigel came here to prevent Mother from killing Jax and Laini. As you can see, both men died in the process."

"Oh, boy. Yes, we have a lot to discuss. Look, I have organized for Laini and Jax to leave via the service elevator before the place is filled with law enforcement. Nigel has already been moved along with that nurse." Daddy glances at his watch. "Someone should be here shortly to move Johnny. No one outside of us will know he was ever here. Then once the medics and police arrive, the coroner will officially declare your mother dead. Not just your mother's death but also Nigel and Johnny will come under FBI jurisdiction."

I nod. "Okay, Daddy." I give him a hug.

"Essy, all the medical equipment will be transferred to your apartment downstairs. We are running out of time to transport it away from the building."

"That is fine. I'll let my people know."

"Listen to me when I say, you must take the children, Jax and Laini, somewhere safe. You must protect them at all costs."

"Okay, Daddy. You can count on me. I'll let Jax know we're leaving. Then I have to grab some of my files from your office and pack some clothes for the baby."

"Okay, but be quick."

"I'll be five minutes."

"Oh, and Essy."

"Yes, Daddy."

"Heads up. We have to make it look as if there was a mafia incident or something."

I nod again and leave Dad in the lounge area.

As fast as I could, I informed Jax we were leaving and to be prepared to go. I pull my cell from my pocket and begin texting Dekk. Requesting his jet be fueled and ready for take-off.

A few of my valued team members arrived ten minutes ago to assist. My medical expert, Stacy, had once been a full G.I. Joe with specialist training as a qualified doctor, came in and began removing the cables attached to Laini.

"Thanks, Stacy. We appreciate everything you're able to do."

Stacy gave me a brief chin lift in acknowledgment while she worked. I will definitely give her a pay raise.

As I rush to my mother's office, my cell vibrates.

I slide it from my pocket and swipe at the screen. Dekk has replied.

DEKK:

The jet is fueled and on standby. I'll meet you there.

I reply back.

ME:

Thanks, honey. Going to be a full crew.

Next, I notify my staff, protecting the children, to take the van straight to the jet.

I switch my cell for my mother's keys from my pocket and quickly remove the hard copy files, a laptop, external hard drives, and a few other items Mother had said for me to take. I store everything in her laptop case and zip it up. Thankfully, my kids and Emma's passports are still here after they traveled with my parents to France earlier this year. I must have unconsciously known something might happen, as I had also organized a passport for Jack just after his birth. I'm glad I had.

I then proceed to baby Jack's room and grab his carry bag, filling it with his baby clothing and anything else we would require, including a couple of tins of baby formula, his baby bottles, bottle cleaning equipment, and a couple of bags of diapers.

As I rush back to Laini, the room she occupied has been emptied — All evidence of her recuperation removed. I quickly place the baby carry bag and the laptop case in the under-bed storage area and hold on to Laini's hand, giving it a slight squeeze.

"We're leaving, Laini. Major shit is about to go down." I release her hand as Stacy pushes the wheeled bed through the door with a couple of portable monitors on the end of the bed.

My other team member, Thomas, has the service elevator ready for us to enter. I walk beside Jax and nod at him. A couple of my father's team, removing their gloves, joined us. Thankfully, there is enough room for all of us in the elevator.

I frown at Henderson and Davies. He nods and murmurs, "The place now looks as if there was a scuffle, and your mother was slaughtered."

Wow. The boys were quick. I give Davies a quick nod.

"Is everyone downstairs in my apartment and leaving spontaneously?"

Henderson nods. "Yes. Agent Johnny was taken away ten minutes ago. Everyone else vacated to your apartment with all the equipment. From there they'll leave when it is safe to do so. We are the last to leave."

I nod.

I glance at Thomas. "Are you prepared to act as the boss?"

Thomas nods. "Yes. As far as anyone is concerned, you're away on assignment." Good. We all require a cover story.

"Thanks, Thomas."

Just as the doors begin to close on the service elevator, I hear my father's agonizing screams for his wife to come back and don't die, followed by loud voices acknowledging the paramedics and police are there.

Now that was close.

Chapter Thirty-Eight

LAINI

The faint sound of beeping alerts me I'm awake. Pressure around my hand informs me someone is holding my hand.

My eyelids slowly flutter, allowing dim light to penetrate my eyeballs. Not sure if that was a good thing or not.

Once I focus, I glance down and notice the top of a head — hair the same color as my husband's — beside me. I take in a deep breath. I need to kick-start my brain. Where am I? As I glance around the room, nothing seems familiar. Nothing at all.

The sound of a baby's cry alerts me to a memory I should know. Then, before I can prevent it, my mind overflows. Memories bombard my head. Events. People. Conversations. Images. With the overload of information swirling around in my head, my temples pulse with an oncoming headache. It might be hours, minutes or seconds but it finally settles, and I glance around again.

Where am I? And more importantly, where is everyone?

Then it dawns on me. I glance back down. Then it clicks, and I smile.

I am back inside my body. I'm alive — whole flesh and blood. No more floating around as a spirit ghost.

I wiggle my toes. A scratching noise sounds as my toenails scrape the sheet. Relief fills me, feeling my toes move back and forth. Next, I try to move my hand, and it will not budge. I frown until I remember Jax is holding on tight.

So instead, I try my vocal cords.

"J...Ja...Jax," I finally manage to get out on a croak. Wow! My vocal cords have not been used for a long time. I don't know how loud I am, but at least I have spoken my first word. My tongue sweeps across my dry lips. Boy, do I need a drink. I try again to call out, "J. Ja. Jax... Jax, wake up," I croak and pull on my hand.

The head of the hair beside me begins to move. "Jax," I croaked again.

Ever so slowly, I watch my husband move enough and sit up in his chair, releasing my hand.

"Jax," I garble. "Drink." My mouth and throat feel dry like a desert.

Super-fast, Jax turns his head with wide eyes toward me. How he didn't give himself whiplash, I do not know.

"Laini...Laini, you're awake."

I smile and nod. "D. Dri. Drink, Jax," I croak.

"Oh, sure. Yeah, babe." He stands and reaches for one of several bottles of water on the nightstand near the bed. He cracks the lid and then places a straw in the open bottle. "Here, babe. Only take a few sips." Ever so slowly, I wrap my lips around the thin straw and then suck.

Somehow, I knew not to gulp the water down. The refreshing water swishes around my mouth before I swallow it. Then another small amount, roll my tongue around, swallow, and sigh. That feels better.

Jax places the bottle beside me on the little side table. I wait for him to say something, but he just stares at me with a smile.

I roll my eyes at him and smile back.

"Jax, where are we?"

His eyes widen, and then he takes in a deep breath.

"What do you remember?"

"I'm not sure. Maybe everything?"

"Laini, that is not an answer."

"I remember being a spirit ghost. My mother is dead. And we have a baby son to love. Now tell me what has happened, and where are we?"

He nods, leans forward, brushes his lips against mine, and then stands. "Before we get into what has happened, I need to let your sister know you're awake. I'll be back in a minute."

I shake my head and watch him walk to the door. He pauses and glances over his shoulder. He probably thinks he's hallucinating. He smiles again and opens the door. The sound of a baby crying reaches my ears. Then, Jax has the door closed behind him.

After several seconds or more, the door opens to reveal a woman I remember as one of my sister's team...Stacy. If I remember rightly, she is not just a marine but also a trained doctor.

"Hello, Stacy."

The woman smiles at me, then checks the machines behind the bed.

"It is good to see you're awake, Laini. At least I now know you have your memories."

"Yes, I think so. I won't know until I am asked questions."

"The standard first questions I know you will not be able to answer," she says and smiles. I frown. I don't understand. "The questions are. Do you know your name? Do you know where you are? And do you know what day it is?"

I nod. "Yes, now I understand. Yes, I know my name is Laini. I am married to Jax. We have a daughter, Emma, and a son, Jack."

"Very good," she replies.

"As for the day, and where? No. I have no idea."

"That is understandable. You have been unconscious for a long time."

"How long is long?"

Before Stacy replies, my daughter bursts into the room, stops, and stares at me with wide eyes.

I smile and feel my eyes mist up. "Baby girl. I have missed you so much."

"Momma," Emma screams and rushes onto the bed, throwing her arms around me in a tight squeeze and pushing the air out of my body. "I knew you would come back to me."

"I was determined, Emma, to come back to you,

your father, and baby Jacky," I say with a smile. "Now, where is your baby brother? I would love to meet him officially."

Emma sits up and wipes the happy tears from her face. "I have missed you so much, Momma. A lot has happened." I nod at her words.

"I know, Em. I know. Is your Aunt Essy here?"

"She sure is," my sister's voice sounds from the doorway. I glance up, and she is, holding my son in her arms. "I think you might like to meet this little guy."

"Essy. It is good to see you."

Her grin is infectious, and her eyes are misting up with tears. "It's good to see you whole and awake."

I nod. "It's good to be awake. Now bring the little man over here."

With a smile from ear to ear, Emma moves to the chair and begins bouncing in her seat with excitement. My sister approaches the bed and carefully places Jack against me. I frown when I realize my arms feel weak— they are not fully functional.

"What is it, Laini?"

"My arms are not moving as they should. I feel weak."

"Well, that is understandable. It has been over eight weeks since the accident."

"What?"

Essy lifts Jack and turns him so he is leaning safely against my front.

"He has grown so much."

"Yes, he has. I made sure Emma took photos of him every day so you would not have completely missed everything when you woke up." I look up at my sister and daughter and smile.

"Thank you, guys. That was thoughtful."

My son continues to sleep. Essy picks him up and passes him to Emma.

"Em, please take Jacky to his room and place him in his bed."

Emma looks like a natural holding the baby. "I'll be back later, Momma. I know you have adult stuff to discuss with Aunt Essy."

My girl is clever. I smile and say, "Thank you, sweetheart. Most appreciative."

"Emma, close the door after you, please."

"Yes, Aunt Essy."

Stacy moves to my side, listens to my heart and lungs, and then checks my eyes and arms, followed by my legs. After a minute or so of lifting, tapping, pulling, pushing, squeezing, and lifting some more, she looks me in the eye and declares, "Laini, with exercise, your strength in your arms and legs will return. But I think you need to adjust to resting before slowly applying some physiotherapy." I nod. I gathered that. No running for me for a week or more. "Now for the unpleasant part."

I frown. What is Stacy speaking of? She sets a medical tray on the side table, then places fresh medical gloves. She checks and palpitates my belly. Then, the bit I was not ready for, she carefully removes a catheter I didn't realize had been inserted.

Oh, boy. My breath freezes as I watch a tube increase in length until it is completely released from my body. Holy, color me in rainbow colors. "Stacy, usually I request dinner and drinks before anyone approaches me there." She laughs, shakes her head, and then removes the intravenous drip from my arm and tacks a small piece of gauze to the site before covering my legs with my sheet up to my waist.

"You owe me dinner at the local restaurant when you're up to it," she says with a smile. She tidies and cleans everything from her tray, placing everything in a trash bag, including her medical gloves. "Make sure you sip plenty of water. I'll be back later to check on you," she says over her shoulder as she leaves the room with the bag.

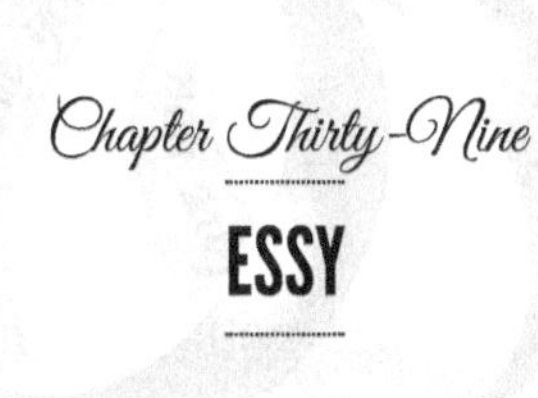

Relief fills me at last. It is so good to see my sister conscious and talking.

For a while there, I thought I would never see her like this again.

"Essy, come on, we are alone now, so spill. Start talking, sister," Laini demands, with a twitch of her lips.

"What do you remember?"

Her eyes pull together in thought before they meet mine with a smile. "First, I woke standing in the hospital and saw my body. Joining you on a mission to find Jax. Entering the hotel room where Jax had stayed before the accident."

"What else do you remember?"

"A lot. Nigel at my holiday house. Finding Jax. Our mother and the Apolo Syndicate. What I would like to know is what happened to her at the penthouse?"

I nod at Laini. Yes. Mother. Now, that is a long story. I shake my head and say, "Where to start?"

"Before you begin there, I want to know where we are and how we got here."

"Now that I can answer. We left our parent's penthouse apartment before law enforcement arrived." Oh, poor daddy, stuck with everything. "We joined with the children at the airport." Thank goodness my team picked up the kid's bags with essential items before arriving at the airport.

"So, we traveled in the jet. I contacted Missy. She was back in the States checking on her business and business partner. Yes, her business partner is Betsy and Johnny's daughter."

"We had figured as much. Our world is far too small. So why did you mention Missy?"

"The reason is, thanks to her husband Tanner, we changed jets back in the U.S. He flew us all to Australia."

"What? Are you saying we are in Australia right now?"

"Yes. We are at a private property in Queensland, Australia."

"Seriously?"

"Yes. Seriously. We've been here for two weeks."

"You have to be kidding me," she says with raised brows.

"No. By staying here, we have remained out of the spotlight. No one knows we are here. Not even father."

"Did Missy and Tanner arrive with us here?"

I nod. "They had for the first week and arranged for our clothing and food to be delivered."

"So where exactly are...." My ind begins spinning

with snippets of information. Places around the world, until my brain registers Missy and her love of... My eyes meet Essy's and her face lights up. "Queensland. Missy. I've got it! We're on Hamilton Island. Missy has always loved this island."

I nod. "See, you still have it."

"Yes, I do," she gloats.

With lunch complete, I help Laini in the shower, with her sitting on a shower chair. We talk about little things and also everything regarding the children. We cover how Missy and Tanner convinced us to stay here, away from the public eye and waited for her to wake up.

"Essy, are you going to fill me in on what happened with Dad, Mom, and Pedro Apolo from the Apolo Syndicate?"

Hairy monkey balls. I had hoped she had forgotten about them.

After I debate what to say, I begin with our father.

"Dad and his team had removed Nigel, Johnny, and the fake nurse from the apartment. Nigel and Johny both had a full honors funeral. Their cause of death was shot in the line of duty and their file had been sealed, so no one will ever know the truth of what really happened."

"Wow. Nigel had been working undercover for a lot

of years. Even I had thought he was a traitor until he explained what had happened and how he organized a young woman's body to be passed off as mine when my birth parents had been murdered."

I forgot how much information Laini had gathered while in her ghostly spirit form.

"You know more details than I do, as Dad would not go into detail with me."

"Becoming a spirit ghost did have its advantages."

"Yes, it had. Laini, can you remember the day of the accident?"

She squints and closes her eyes. I can see she is trying to remember. She shakes her head her eyes open and meets mine. "The more I try the more it remains the same. Blank. Whatever happened to Jax and me on the day he was taken, is still a mystery. I wonder if my brain is protecting my mind from the horrific events."

I nod. "Most likely. What happened to you, all the trauma is not something you ever want to relive or remember."

One thing I have noticed is the tone and attitude when Laini speaks. My senses are warning me there is something not right. My heart says, *'Give her a break. She just woke up!'* It might be a side effect of the coma.

For now, I'll watch and see how she goes.

Chapter Forty

LAINI

"We'll discuss the other details later after we play catch up. Now, what about that nurse who tried to kill me?" That woman was a bitch. Who waits and follows orders to kill a helpless unconscious woman and a baby. I could have been killed at any moment. She could have killed my son, just as the other woman attempted.

Essy's voice interrupts my internal rant, "Yes, the Syndicate spy, who played nurse, well, she was taken to the morgue as a Jane Doe. The bullet in her head will not match my ammunition or come from any of my weapons." Whoa. At least, that is something. Thank goodness for our family with high and secret connections.

"How was Dad? What happened when the police arrived?"

Essy shakes her head.

Why is she shaking her head? What happened?

"Brief version. Some of my and Dad's team had

arranged the apartment to seem as if there had been a scuffle and an execution-style murder. Not sure why, but Johnny had carried one of his father's old hitmen's guns. Thankfully, he did. It has been written up as the murder weapon."

"Does that mean mother's death was treated as a homicide and not self-defense?" What a mess.

"Yes. It was made to look like there was someone else in the apartment. Father had also convinced the detective on duty that he arrived home looking for his wife when she failed to meet him for lunch. Dad had one of my people organize a booking for two at one of their favorite restaurants. Covering their bases."

"So, your people hacked the restaurant's computer system, inserting our parents' booking."

"Basically, yes."

"How is Dad?"

"He's grieving, of course, but he explained that he has been undercover from the start. The FBI and CIA had discovered our mother's background and kept her under watch. Our parents loved one another in their own way. And Dad reminded me he loves us with his whole heart and soul." At least, that is something. We have two parents who loved us in their own way.

Then I think of Susanna and what she said. "Mother told me that if everything went wrong, the nurse had been given orders to kill us. Our mother never wanted Pedro Apolo to get his hands on either of us or our family. For she knew he would manipulate us for his own gain."

"Well, at least we no longer have to worry about Pedro Apolo."

Huh? What have I missed? "Why? What do you mean?"

"Pedro was taken into custody. Thanks to all the evidence our mother had kept over the years, the Apolo Syndicate was taken down, and their assets seized. Two days ago, while Pedro was being transferred to court, he was shot in the head, killing him instantly. His grandson Paulie was also shot and died a few hours later."

"What happened to Philip?"

"Now, that is the interesting part. It turns out Philip had joined Johnny as a government agent. Pedro had turned his grandsons against their father when Pedro had Philip's wife killed. Pedro also had Philips' first-born daughter taken and killed when she was five years old to keep Philip in line."

"You have to be joking. Why would anyone have a child killed?"

"I suppose the same thing happened when Pedro made sure our mother had miscarried with our first brother. She never knew the new doctor she had been seeing was under Pedro's thumb. He could have saved the baby but allowed the fetus to die by his hand."

"How tragic. Speaking of brothers, have you spoken to our lost biological brother?"

"No, not personally, anyway. I emailed him to confirm he has an interview with my team in the near future when he's back stateside. So even if he is not our brother, he will have a job if he passes our testing program.”

“You are hesitant about him?”

“Laini, after all the lies in our family, I am not rushing anything. Once he is in my employ, I will have him DNA tested.”

“Sneaky, but required.”

“Yes. Very.”

“So why are we still here in hiding?”

“As I said, the Apolo Syndicate was taken down. But, with his family members and some of Pedro’s hit men still out and about, it is wise to remain here for a little while longer.”

I nod. Okay, now for the next awkward question regarding our mother.

“Essy, has Momma been buried?”

Essy pauses. I can see she is contemplating her answer. “Sis, Dad had mother cremated. One of my team members has flown to Australia and couriered her ashes here. Dad wanted the both of us to do something regarding Mother.”

Well, then. That answers that. I nod, and Essy continues to towel dry my hair.

Chapter Forty-One

LAINI

My restless days have turned into several busy weeks.

Little by little, I regained my strength and the full function of my body. Jax has remained by my side. Even though it has started to get a bit frustrating, Jax, has been enthusiastic regarding my physio. I don't know who's more eager for me to be back at full strength and movement. He's even encouraging me with my writing. Making sure I have everything I need for my notebook computer. At least he is constant in what he is doing, he wants his wife back. I agree, I want me back as well, and to be a mother to my kids. He even surprises me every day with a treat or an outing, when I notice the love in his eyes each time he sees me smile melts my heart.

Today he's taking me to lunch. I think he said it was a picnic in a quiet secluded spot he's discovered on the island. I love being able to spend physical time with my husband. We have a lot of lost time to make up for.

As for my baby son, Jack, he knows who I am and smiles at me every chance he's has. He is no longer my newborn, he's growing like a bean. I've had to order new baby clothes for him. Jack has outgrown everything we had. He loves being in the water and splashing around. Jax has been taking him to swimming lessons. I thought Jack was far too young, but the instructor informed Jax it was never too early for children to learn. It may just save my boy's life.

Emma has grown so much before my eyes. No longer my little girl, she has grown into a beautiful young woman. Spending so much time away from school, I was going to organize homeschooling for her, only to discover Essy had already taken care of it back when we were in the States. Thank goodness for my sister.

We have been one huge happy family here at Hamilton Island. Our food shopping, which we order online, is delivered every week. Essy and Dekk have purchased a big boat, sorry, one of those luxury yachts.

It's brilliant. We can go out on the ocean and still feel as if we are home. The surrounding islands, white sand beaches, and coral reefs are beautiful to see. I've even enjoyed a few days out on the water without the kids.

Since waking, my mind has been busy with all the different aspects and details. Such things would never allow an author's mind to rest or be alone. So, with my laptop computer and the creative juices flowing, I've started tapping out a new romance book. Well, two of them.

One I have written around Betsy and Johnny. A mafia romance. The other is a murder mystery romance, with bits and pieces from my own family's history included. This morning I sent them off to my editor. If she likes them and I approve her recommendations and changes, I'll send them off to my agent to approach the publishing house.

With the sun shining down, warming my sun-kissed skin, I laze back, enjoying life.

"Laini, are you ready?"

My eyes snap open to Jax's voice. I must have dozed off and smile at my gorgeous husband.

"So, my husband, where are we going today for our picnic?"

"It's a surprise. But, I will say we are headed to the marina."

"Why the marina?"

"You'll have to wait and see," he cheekily says. With a caress of his hand along my shoulder, he then places his hand under my chin and lifts it. He leans forward and brushes my lips with his. "Come on, if we don't leave now, our food will spoil."

I frown at his words and wonder where we are going. Something inside my head is getting sick of his games. Normally I love it when Jax surprises. Is there something wrong with me? Or do I just require a change of scenery?

"You know, this sand is going to find itself in places sand should never go."

Fine white sand particles slip through my fingers. Water laps around our feet at the shore's edge as the tide slowly closes in on our naked bodies as we enjoy the afternoon sunshine on a deserted beach in the Whitsundays.

"Laini, it's not my fault. I cannot resist you. If and when I have the chance to make love to you, I will. I love you, my beautiful wife," Jax says as he brushes his lips over my shoulder and down my chest.

"I love you, too, my sexy husband." I release a moan and arch against Jax's talented mouth.

He lifts his lips long enough to say, "You know, it feels good. To finally have that plaster cast off my leg. Finally, able to have a shower without a shower bag cover over the top of it."

With my head thrown back, enjoying his ministrations, I murmur, "Yes, good. Shower."

"The best part is able to make love to you without the cast getting in our way."

"Yes. I can totally agree with that."

Jax positions himself back between my thighs and thrusts forward, stretching and filling me completely. We release a moan as Jax speeds up. One of his hands reaches between us as his fingers stroke my bundle of nerves in a rhythmic motion, adding just the right amount of pressure I like.

My fingernails scratch along his back and shoulders,

and my heels press against his flexing butt cheeks. It is not long before the telltale sign of my approaching orgasm. With my inner muscles tightening, my orgasm hits as my channel flutters and pulses with the feeling of utopia sweeping through me as my back arches and my toes flex and wiggle.

My rushed breaths puff by Jax's ear as he surges forward and bucks against me as his hard cock expands and pulses just before his release bursts free. He grunts and wiggles his hips before collapsing on top of me.

With his chest heaving, and his heart pounding he mutters, "Boy, am I unfit," beside my ear. "I definitely have to work on my fitness." All I can do is nod. Fit or not, my speaking ability is not possible right now.

When the water reaches our thighs, we know it is time to move.

"Jax, we better move."

With a heave and grunt. Jax rolls over to my side and sprawls out. "Yeah, yeah. In a minute. I need to catch my breath first." I shake my head. Oh, my poor husband, he's getting old! "Laini, it takes a lot to make sure you are satisfied. If I'm going to do a job, I must make sure I accomplish it right every time."

I burst out laughing. "Jax, you're lucky I love you so much. Come on, sit up. It's time to go for an afternoon swim before we leave."

We take our time swimming and snorkeling in the warm ocean water. Under the water, we enjoy watching the fish swim about while looking at the different species of coral.

Once back to shore, we slip into our bathing outfits.

Jax assists, tying my string bikini behind my neck before reaching for the com unit to contact the boat to come back to our private cove to pick us up. We place our towels, cells, drink bottles, sunscreen, beach shoes, and the com unit back in the waterproof bag before placing them with our picnic hamper and snorkel equipment back in the floating container.

"Give the boat five minutes or so to make its way back to us. The captain said he'll come close enough for us to swim back to the boat."

"Looks like we might as well place our flippers back on."

"Sounds like a plan. It would make it easier to reach them."

We pull the flippers from the container and head to the water's edge. We slip our flippers on and make our way into deeper water. It doesn't take long for the boat to meet us. They grab our equipment as we climb on board, slipping off our flippers.

"How was the water?" one of the deck crew asks as he heaves the container with our belongings onto the deck.

"Fantastic. I'll never tire of watching the fish swim around the coral," I say as I reach for my towel out of the bag.

The sound of rushing water reaches my ears. I glance up to see Jax hosing himself off under the shower spray. I join him and rinse the salt and sand away. Dripping wet, I wrap my towel around my body and sit on a bench seat as Jax joins me and wraps his arm around my shoulders.

"I love you, Laini."

I smile at Jax. My heart fills with joy and love whenever I look at him.

"I love you, my sexy husband." And kiss his gorgeous lips.

Jax deepens our kiss before slowly pulling away and smiling at me. I lean my head against his shoulder and watch the scenery go by as we make our way back to the marina at Hamilton Island.

The peace, quiet, and freedom over the last couple of months have been fantastic.

If only we could live here forever!

Chapter Forty-Two

LAINI

"**M**issy, it is so good to see you," I mutter with my hand over my mouth. The urge to throw up increases with each second. Why is she here, of all things? I feel like crap.

Huh?

I shake my head at the hurtful thoughts. What has gotten into me?

Opening the front door to my new house — A relief now that we are no longer sharing Missy's house. As I eye Missy, saliva pools in my mouth. That is not a good sign. Come to think of it, whatever we ate last night has not agreed with me.

"Geez, girl. Hello to you too. Why do you like shit?"

I shake my head and slowly swallow. I would have felt insulted if I didn't love her as I do. Second thoughts — I do feel insulted.

Where are these bad thoughts and words coming from?

"I don't feel so good. I think it was something I ate yesterday," I reply, attempting to sound normal.

Missy eyes me up and down with a raised brow. Then, before she can say a word, Essy walks up behind her.

"Missy, what are you doing here? I thought you were staying in the States for another week or two."

Staying here as long as we have, it did not take Essy and me long to both agree to purchase a house here on Hamilton Island. Who wouldn't? This place is beautiful. Plus, with real estate prices crashing, we were at the right place at the right time. Somehow, Essy purchased the house next door to mine in Plum Pudding Close. Color me in rainbow colors. Thinking of food is not the best for me right now.

We started on upgrades and extensions as soon as the new houses were legally in our names. We love Missy and Tanner and appreciate everything they have done, but we no longer want to be a burden to them.

In our tropical hideaway houses, we both have five bedrooms, four bathrooms, a large kitchen, dining area, and lounge, as well as fantastic outdoor entertaining areas with infinity pools and an outdoor spa. Jax, the kids, and I moved in over a week ago, and Essy, Dekk, and their children moved into theirs a few days ago, allowing Missy and Tanner to have their holiday home back.

Currently, we have a deck and walkway being built between the properties. It will save us the hassle of walking to the front door of either house once it's complete. Also, it will make it more private for both our families. The upside being in this location on the island, we have less foot and vehicle traffic.

Before she can answer, Tanner appears behind the girls. "Hello, ladies," he says with a smile. "Where are the boys?"

"Over at Dent Island playing golf with a few others," Essy answers.

"I'll see you later, ladies. Babe, you going to be okay if I take the buggy?"

Missy rolls her eyes at Tanner and smiles. "Of course, Adrian. If you're returning to the house, can you ensure your parents are okay looking after the kids and let them know where I am?"

As a friend, we all call Adrian by his nickname — Tanner. Missy and his parents call him Adrian. As for his business associates, they know him as Mr. Steele, and the few who may call him Adrian. Sometimes his name can become a little confusing to some of his friends.

Tanner leans forward with his brow raised and whispers something in Missy's ear. She giggles and shakes her head. I barely hear his next words. "Are you sure?"

Missy nods her head and smiles.

I wonder what they are speaking about?

Tanner then kisses his wife's lips, waves at us, then slips his cell out of his cargo shorts pocket. He must be phoning the boys.

Typical. Boys and golf.

It looks like Missy is staying. So, I step back and allow Missy and Essy to enter.

"Wow, Laini, the house looks fantastic," she announces as she looks around my bright, sunshine-filled house. Then, she turns to Essy and asks, "How's everything with yours? All settled in."

We head for the kitchen. I grab a soda bottle out of the drink's refrigerator. Essy and Missy grab a bottle of mineral water, crack the lid, and take a mouthful. From the pantry, I reach for a packet of crackers from the overhead cupboard. All I have to do is act nice and speak politely. Basically, act normal. If only I didn't feel so blah. It doesn't take me long to fill the bowel.

After swallowing her mouthful, Essy replies, "Yes, thanks. We couldn't have picked a better house. We added many modern features and upgrades, just as Laini has."

I offer the girls the bowl of crackers, which they don't hesitate, and select several, shoving them in their mouths.

"Thanks," Essy and Missy nod and mumble around a mouthful of crackers.

Once Essy finishes her mouthful, she continues, "We came to the conclusion that if you're going to be staying here for a large amount of time, it is best to make everything to our liking."

Missy nods. "I agree. As you would have seen from my holiday house, we made all our upgrades and changes ready for any occasion."

We sit on the sun lounges with an extra drink on the balcony overlooking the blue tropical water views.

My stomach finally settles while eating the dry

crackers. I lean back, enjoying the warm tropical weather.

"Hey, Missy. What was Tanner quietly asking you before he left?" Essy questions.

I look over at her, and she shrugs her shoulders, then raises her brow. "I don't know what is going on with him lately." She pauses and shakes her head as if she's in thought. She glances at us and says, "He asked if I have something to tell him. I've got no idea what he's going on about?"

"What a strange thing to ask! Has Tanner remained faithful to you? No visits to his club?" I ask.

"What? No. If Adrian were to visit a club, he would take me. No, he is acting strange, that's all."

Missy glances at Essy and raises her brow. "What about you, Essy? Has Declyn been acting strange to you?" Missy looks at me and once again raises her brow. "What about you, Laini? Has Jaxton said anything, or has his behavior changed from normal?"

I shake my head. But then a thought comes to me.

Chapter Forty-Three

JAXTON

"Hey, my man. Good to see you. Did you bring them?" I ask, shaking Tanner's hand.

Tanner nods, then look at Dekk. "Have you spoken to Essy? Will she require one as well?"

Dekk nods. "I am certain she does even though she does not know."

"Seriously. How do they not know?" I say in amazement. "Come on. We better go. The girls think we are playing golf."

"Yes, well. Essy had said as much. When the girls discover you have not been playing golf... I would not like to be in your shoes," Tanner smugly says.

"We're faithful. We are devoted. Our wives love us. You could say we are spending some quality men bonding time together. Men need shit like that," Dekk says with a smirk.

We all laugh and nod our heads.

"Yes, we do. Now come on. Our women do not have

a clue. And for once, men have more knowledge than a woman.”

“Are you seriously playing with your balls right now? Talk about playing with fire. If our wives heard such words, we would have no sex for weeks, maybe months.”

“Nah. Our wives cannot live without our ability to caress them just the way they like. Our touch fulfills them.”

“Fills them, all right. We are the ones responsible for getting them in the situation they are in.” Dekk cringes.

“Don’t remind me. But at the same time. I cannot wait,” I say. I’ve missed the birth of my two children. This time I’m determined to be there for the whole pregnancy for once.

“Let’s go, boys. Time to confront our wives,” Tanner says.

Chapter Forty-Four

LAINI

The urge to throw up hits me out of the blue when Missy offers me a platter of mixed meats and cheeses. The odor from the spicy meat mixed with the cubed cheese hits my nostrils. I move back away from the platter and cover my mouth.

"Laini, what's wrong? You've turned green."

I shake my head as I get up from my chair and rush to the bathroom.

Essy's voice reaches my ear. "What happened? Why she'd rush off?"

I don't wait around. Instead, I head to the nearest bathroom, straight to the toilet, and lift the seat. Anything I recently consumed comes up and out, splashing into the bowl within seconds.

Landing on my knees and continue to empty my stomach.

Oh, geez. I can't stop. What is wrong with me?

The sound of knocking, followed by Essy's voice, reaches my ears. "Laini, are you okay?"

I shake my head and continue to dry reach.

She steps in behind me. I feel my hair being moved to the side.

"Oh, hairy monkey balls. I gotta go," Essy mumbles.

Before I can ask what she means, she's out the door and gone.

A minute or so later, the door opens wide again.

"Laini, I have a damp cloth for you," Missy murmurs.

I reach back and grab it and mumble, "Thanks." And wipe my clammy face.

The next thing I hear is Missy mumble, "Oh, gods. I'm going to be sick. Sorry, Laini."

The sound of her footsteps can be heard rushing down the hallway.

What has gotten into us? We're mothers. We have stronger stomachs than this. I hope we do not have a stomach bug. Oh, not the kids. I don't think I could handle it if the kids throw up.

Over half an hour later, Essy, Missy, and I sit outside with soda water and a few dry crackers.

"How are you two feeling now?" I manage to say around chewing on another cracker.

"I've been better," Essy mumbles, still looking a little green.

"So have I. What do you think caused us to be sick?" Missy groans as she takes another sip of her drink.

"I don't know, but we better find out. I hope the kids don't catch or have it," I groan out.

"Oh, no. Don't say that. I couldn't handle them spewing. Especially the way I feel at the moment," Essy mumbles.

"I don't know about you. I need to sleep for a bit," Missy says with a yawn.

I nod. "I agree."

We all roll onto our sides and attempt to doze.

My husband's voice breaks through the sleepy fog I prefer to remain in.

"Laini, come on. I'll take you to bed." My body is lifted.

I shake my head and moan, "No. Leave me here." My husbands aftershave fills my nostrils and I snuggle into his chest.

"No, babe. You're going to bed where it is more comfortable."

"Check the kids." Something cool touches my back, followed by the softness of my mattress. My bed. Just what I need and rollover. Ahhh. My stomach begins to roll. Not again. Just wait until I discover which kid gave me their sick germs. "Make sure they don't have what I've got," I moan.

The last thing I hear is, "Somehow, I don't think they will, babe." I didn't hear anything else as darkness takes over.

Chapter Forty-Five

LAINI

Somewhere in my sleeping subconscious. I swear someone is calling my name.

'Laini pet. Wake up. We need to speak with you.'

Huh? I would say Betsy was here if my brain was not so foggy.

Betsy!

My eyelids snap open as I sit up. Moving far too quickly has me covering my mouth once more.

Bugger. No.

I scramble out of my bed and rush to my bathroom and begin dry reaching. What feels like minutes or hours, my stomach muscles protest with its rough treatment. There is nothing left in it to bring anything up apart from froth.

Arhhh. Why me?

I sit on the floor with my back against the wall and reach above my head for a towel from the rail to wipe my face.

The familiar buzz alerts me. I was not dreaming before, Betsy really is here.

'*Laini pet. What is wrong? Why are you sick?*'

I glance towards her and shrug, and shake my head slowly. '*I have no idea. I think one of the kids might have shared their sick germs.*'

Betsy moves in and takes a closer look at my face. '*Laini pet, when was the last time you menstruated?*'

I frown at the thought. Periods? Then it dawns on me. I don't remember.

'*I have no idea, Betsy. Why?*'

'*Why? I think you might be pregnant again.*'

'*Pregnant.*' I shake my head at the horrid thought. '*No. Not possible.*'

'*Are you sure? You have that look, Laini pet.*'

My eyes meet her concerned ones. '*What look? I do not have a look.*'

She smiles and nods. '*You do, Laini pet. I have seen that same look each time you've been expecting.*'

I shake my head once again to banish the thought. '*No. Essy and Missy have all been sick with me. We have a virus.*'

Betsy smiles. '*You keep telling yourself, Laini pet. But, mark my words. You're pregnant. And most likely so is Essy and Missy.*'

My eyes bulge at the thought. Are all three of us pregnant? Nah. No way. Definitely not possible.

I must change the topic of conversation before I throw up again. '*Betsy, I am glad to see you are here. Where have you been?*'

I watch Betsy turn and disappear through the door before returning to the bathroom with Johnny.

Fantastic. Visitors and I most likely look like crap.

Johnny smiles down at me and shakes his ghostly head. *'You look like death, Laini. What's going on?'*

'Do not know, Johnny. Now, are you both going to tell me why you're here?' I look from one to the other, waiting for them to speak.

Feeling uncomfortable on the cool hard floor, I slowly stand, flush the toilet, and lean over the vanity to rinse my mouth. Once I feel a little better, I sit back down on the closed toilet seat.

'Laini pet, we are here to say our goodbyes.'

Huh? I frown and shake my head. *'What are you saying? Where are you going?'*

Betsy smiles, looks at Johnny, then back at me. *'We're finalizing our affairs. Which will allow us to move on from this world.'*

What? No. Just no. *'You can't do that. What about me? What about your daughter?'*

'That is why we are here. I need you to complete our last wishes.'

'What happens if I refuse?'

'Laini pet. You only say that because what I said is a shock to you. Once you think about it rationally, you will do as I have asked.'

'But... But. I don't want you to go. You're part of my life.'

'Oh, my Little Laini pet. You will always be a part of me. You're my family, and you will always be.'

I reach up and touch my face to discover tears streaking down my face, and taking in a deep breath. I pause long enough to think rationally. It's time for me to be brave. Betsy couldn't stay with me forever, even though I would prefer if she did, but I know how selfish that is of me.

Filled with sadness, I sigh as my shoulders sag in defeat. *'Betsy, what do you require me to do?'*

She smiles with pride and nods. *'We need you to take some notes for us.'* I nod and slowly stand. Okay, I can do this. I just have to make sure I don't throw up while I do it.

Betsy and Johnny move through my bathroom door into my bedroom. Standing on unsteady feet, I rinse my mouth again and brush my teeth before following Betsy and Johnny into my bedroom and walking straight to my laptop on my side table. If Betsy expects me to take notes, typing them will be a better option.

Leaning back on my bed with my back against the bedhead, I open my laptop and start a blank document, pausing with a raised brow with my fingers hovering over the keys and glancing at Betsy.

'Right, Laini pet. We need you to write the following — Daughter Francine Burton Stelton. Raised by Mr. Landon Burton and Mrs. Wendy Burton. Francine, married for four years. Spouse — Jamie Stelton. One child — Son — James. Part business partner of the USA branch of Missy's — Jamés Advertising.' I smile. Essy and I worked out Francine was Missy's US business partner.

After a few more keystrokes, I glance up from the screen. *'As soon as I heard the name Francine, it clicked to who she might be.'*

Betsy acknowledges. *'Yes. A small world and all. Now, we would like you to add the following.'* I continued typing, documenting every word Betsy and Johnny said. Bank account details. Land title information. Safe deposit box details and where to find it. Johnny's house address, where to find the key and security code to enter his house. Where his wall safe was and the code to open it. *'Now, once you have everything, we would like you to meet our daughter. Go to the U.S. with Missy. Explain to her about her parents and what happened to her birth parents. Let her know we love her.'*

'What will I find in Johnny's house?'

Before I can finish, Johnny cuts in. *'Laini, you need to collect all my personal papers. Gather all the business documents. Make copies if you must. It is important that you get everything as soon as possible. Before my family discovers and takes over my house.'*

'Are you sure?'

'Yes. I have my current will and a list of instructions in the safe. Follow them, please. And complete what I failed to do.'

Then it clicks.

'You have more proof against your family in the wall safe, don't you?'

Johnny smiles and nods. *'Yes.'*

I pause for a second. *'I thought the Apolo Syndicate was brought down?'*

Johnny shakes his head. *'No. Not by a long shot. Fortunately, I have the proof to bring down the bastards and end the Apolo Syndicate once and for all.'*

Okay... He doesn't ask for much.

Chapter Forty-Six

JAXTON

ith Laini sleeping, I head to my home office, where the boys are waiting for me.

"How's Laini?" Tanner asks.

"Green. Her morning sickness has hit. How do I make her feel better?"

Dekk smiles and shakes his head. "That is the million-dollar question. Morning sickness can be extremely bad and tricky to deal with. All you can do is be there for her. Provide some ginger ale and plenty of dry crackers, and most of all, allow her to rest."

"What about Essy and Missy? Are they as sick as Laini?"

Tanner and Declyn look at one another, then at me. "Missy is still feeling nauseous. But, after some rest, she'll bounce back as good as new until tomorrow morning."

Dekk shakes his head again. "Essy is the same. She has no clue why she's feeling the way she is. At the moment, she is resting. Essy is going to explode when she realizes she's pregnant."

"Boys, I think our little three-day getaway a couple of months ago is going to bite us on the ass. I love my wife and kids, but I don't want to face an angry, annoyed woman anytime soon," I say.

The boys nod in agreement. We are so in trouble.

With Tanner's help, Declyn organized a few days out on the water on his new yacht. We basically kidnapped our wives. No kids. No clothes apart from summer robes and bathing suits. Good food and plenty of drinks. A time to relax and enjoy one another.

Which, in hindsight, was not such a good idea. Not thinking we required protection, as our wives were on birth control tablets. Of course, they would have been if the pills weren't left back at the holiday house.

"Come on. We better prepare a little dinner party and the surprise news reveal. Tanner, make sure you have the pregnancy tests handy."

At this very minute, I'm not sure whether to be excited or nervous when Laini discovers she is pregnant. Don't get me wrong. I want to be a father again and enjoy all the pregnancy stuff, including the delivery. With the past two pregnancies, I missed so much with our kids. If I can help it, I never want to miss anything with my family again.

Chapter Forty-Seven

LAINI

Dinner tonight was fantastic. The boys have outdone themselves. A little bit of a variety, and my stomach did not complain. While we girls waited for the boys to complete preparing dinner, I discussed my meeting and sad farewell with Betsy and Johnny.

Essy agreed to leave with me to sneak back into the States and complete the mission. It is a matter of when to leave.

As I lift my glass of water and glance over the rim, I notice the boys silently speaking with one another. What are they up to?

I turn to my sister and ask, "So, Essy. You were saying the twins also had that stomach bug. How is Bella?"

I take another sip of water. Tanner coughs into his hand, and Dekk shakes his head.

I glance at Essy and Missy, and we give one another

a matching look. We've all noticed the boys are acting strangely.

What is happening?

My sister raises her eyebrow, glances at the boys, and then back at us. Missy and I both nod in agreement. Essy is going to confront the boys first.

"So, boys. What are you hiding from us?" Essy says with a straight face.

Missy sits a little taller and follows on. "Yes. What is the special occasion for our dinner party without the kids?"

"Come on. What is going on?" I demand.

We watch the boys all share a look, then a nod.

Tanner is the one to speak first. "Us husbands have noticed something different with you three. We have been waiting patiently for you to say something, but it seems you do not know or are waiting before informing us."

I look to Essy and then to Missy. We shrug our shoulders and shake our heads in confusion.

This time I speak, "Tanner, explain yourself. We have no idea what you're going on about."

Tanner nods to Dekk and Jax. They nod in turn. Next, all three reach for something under the table and place...

"Are you kidding me right now?" Missy demands. Looking at the pregnancy test in front of her. "Why in the world are you showing us a pregnancy test?"

Dekk opens his mouth and glances at his wife before turning back to Missy. "Are you saying you have not suspected you might be pregnant?"

"Me?" Missy screeches.

Tanner nods, then he looks at both Essy and me. "And also you, Laini, and Essy."

My eyes go from Missy to Essy, and we all shake our heads in disbelief before I glance at the box in front of me.

"No," I mumble. "I think you guys are dreaming. We are not pregnant!"

All three men nod their heads and smile. "Yes, you are," Jax says.

"No, we're not," I repeat, even though Betsy was adamant I was pregnant, and I refused to acknowledge the possibility.

Tanner then cuts in. "That is why we have the tests." Jax and Dekk nod and point to the tests. "You can take them tonight or first thing in the morning."

"Are you serious right now, Tanner?" Missy demands. Wow! It is rarely my girl addresses her husband as Tanner. She must be more than pissed with her husband.

"Yes. I am. You're pregnant, Missy, and so are you, Laini, and Essy."

Chapter Forty-Eight

LAINI

When the three of us show one another the test results, they all display the same thing — Positive.

You have to be kidding me!

Far too many emotions ran through my mind until...

"My first question is, how is it that all three of us are pregnant at the same time?" I ask.

Essy glances at Missy, then at me, and shakes her head. "I have no clue. I have been on birth control."

Missy nods her head in agreement. "I am too."

They both look at me, and I shrug.

"I hadn't started taking mine yet. Weaning Jack to drink formula, remember? So my period has not started."

Missy's eyes narrow. I can see she is in deep thought.

"Do you remember those few surprise days away? Who would think of taking their birth control packet with them? It was only meant to be a day trip. Instead, it turned into several days."

Essy nods. "The same here. Who would think of taking their birth control with them on a day trip?"

"Exactly."

"I'm thinking... would the boys plan something this sneaky and low?"

"I don't know. My body is still recovering from my last pregnancy!" I murmur. Then looking at Essy and Missy. "You wouldn't think... Would you?"

The three of us stare at one another, then nod.

"Yes. Yes, they would!" Essy declares.

The boys are in so much trouble right now.

"I don't know about the both of you, but I'm thinking that trip to the States without our husbands is due right about now!"

We all nod in agreement.

Essy glances at me. "Sis, once back in the states, I'll accompany you to the bank and Johnny's house before we meet with Missy and carefully speak with Francine."

"Thank you. Yes. I think that will be best." I turn to Missy. "Do you agree? We have to be careful when dealing with Francine."

She nods. "Yes. This will blow her world by discovering her biological parents are dead."

I nod. Essy and I know just how she will feel. We've been there. It was more than a shock when Essy and I discovered our adoptive parents were our biological parents. Their long-lost embryos.

My sister's voice grabs my attention. "Laini, it will be best to contact dad from the plane to arrange a meeting. What we have to discuss is too dangerous to speak over the phone. The destruction of the Apolo Syndicate will shake the mafia to its core."

"You can say that again." The government agencies are going to be busy with crime gangs.

I watch Missy remove her cell from her pocket. "If your calendar is like mine, you'll have several meetings you cannot postpone."

"Yes. My schedule is at the point I have to appear in person. Too many meetings," Essy says.

I nod. "I agree. I have to meet my editor and agent regarding the two manuscripts I recently sent them."

"That is that, then. I'll place the call to the pilot to prepare the jet for takeoff tonight." She glances at both Essy and me. "Time to pack your bags, ladies, and grab your passports."

Chapter Forty-Nine

JAXTON

In all my life, this has been the most nerve-racking experience. Confronting our wives with the news, we have suspected, as our wives had blissfully ignored all the symptoms.

It had taken some convincing, but we men stuck to our guns and encouraged the girls to take the tests. So here we are, sitting patiently in the lounge area overlooking the water, waiting.

"What is taking them so long?" Dekk whines. "How long does it take to piss on a stick?"

"I bet they're using both tests and freaking out about it once they had seen positive on the first test," Tanner announces.

As for me, this is the first time I have been in this position. I missed everything with my daughter, Emma. I missed far too much of the pregnancy with Jack. This time, things will be different. I will be there every step of the way with my gorgeous wife.

Hushed voices sound from the hallway. Good, the girls are on their way back.

"Here we go," I whisper as I look at Tanner and Declyn. They grin and nod.

"Remember to remain diplomatic, supporting, and loving," Tanner whispers back.

The girls appear with straight faces. They are going to make us wait. It's silly, though. We already know that they are pregnant, but we'll play along.

My eyes focus on Laini, and I smile at her beautiful face and mouth. *'I love you.'*

She doesn't smile back, which wipes my smile from my face.

What's wrong?

Why isn't she smiling back at me?

I stand and go straight to her.

Both Tanner and Declyn do the same with their wives.

"Laini, what is it? What is wrong?"

Her eyes narrow at me.

Uh-oh.

"Jaxton." I cringe at her tone. Laini only says my full name when angry or upset with me. Why is she upset?

"Adrian Steele, care to explain how the three of us girls are pregnant?" Missy demands.

My focus moves from Laini to Missy.

Missy just announced that they were pregnant. All three of them are pregnant.

I watch Tanner and Declyn smile at their wives, pulling them into their arms from the corner of my eye as I engulf Laini in my arms.

I hear Tanner reply, "Um. Sex usually helps."

With my pregnant wife against my body, I want to jump for joy.

"Laini, I love you." And attempt to kiss my wife.

She turns her head to the side, wiggles in my arms, and pushes against my chest, causing me to take a step back.

What? What is wrong? Isn't she happy? I am. I'm ecstatic with joy and love.

I'm going to be a father!

I step away from Jax. So do Essy and Missy from their husbands.

Our husbands stand there mute as a statue.

"Before you say a word. Essy, Missy, and I have prior plans. In half an hour, the three of us will leave to return to the States for business. You'll be remaining here with the kids," I declare. Both Essy and Missy nod in agreement.

"Babe, we'll go with you," Dekk pleads.

Essy shakes her head. "No. What Laini and I have to do cannot wait. It is safer to leave the kids here with you. We have unfinished business to take care of. Plus, we have business meetings we can no longer avoid."

"Missy, are you intending to use my jet?"

Missy stills, then glares at her husband. "I'll be using our jet, Adrian. If I require using it. I will." She then turns and says over her shoulder, "I'll see you, girls, at the airport." Then she storms out of the room.

"Shit," Tanner blurts out and takes off after his wife.

Essy smiles at me and says, "I'll meet you there." Then she, too, walks out of my house for her own.

Dekk grumbles under his breath and follows his wife, leaving Jax and me alone.

"Do you hate me, Laini?" my husband quietly states.

I turn back to him, seeing the hurt and anguish in his eyes.

"I'm disappointed, Jax." And begin walking toward our bedroom to pack a small bag. The sound of footsteps behind me lets me know Jax is following me. "Why didn't you speak to me first, Jax? Why did you and the guys gang up on us?"

"I don't know, Laini. Tanner and Dekk had wondered why your sister and Missy had mentioned nothing. So, we waited. And well... we could have handled the whole situation better."

"Yes. You could have," I say as I place several items in my overnight bag. It does not take me long to pack what I require. I grab my laptop, passport, and several other things, packing them in my bags.

I turn to face Jax. He looks heartbroken. "Jax, I love you. But I am extremely disappointed. I don't know how I feel about being pregnant. The same for my sister and Missy. We have some serious thinking to do on the plane."

Jax snaps his head up. "What do you mean by *serious thinking*? We are keeping the baby, aren't we?"

I shake my head. "I don't know, Jax. We had a baby several months ago. I don't know if I want to go through with another pregnancy."

"What? No. I want this baby, Laini. I want to be

there with you at every turn. I never want to miss a thing."

"That is just it, Jax. We never discussed having another baby at our age. I... I. Look, I am going to think about it, okay?"

I kiss my husband on the cheek and walk out the door with my bags.

Chapter Fifty-One

LAINI

We say our emotional goodbyes to our children. Between Essy, Missy, and I, our kids were reluctant for us to leave. I bet the boys had spoken to our kids. Why would our children suddenly have issues when they know we are hard-working women?

Missy had Neil organize our itinerary from a business point of view, including accommodation. Neil also set up a business meeting with Francine in the New York office.

If anyone were watching us, all they would see were three businesswomen attending meetings.

As for our husbands... They have found themselves out in the proverbial doghouse. Acting like cavemen, our husbands were against the three of us traveling without them. Essy gave our husbands her *'don't piss me off'* look, and our men soon stepped back, allowing us to board the jet.

If Jax, Declyn, and Tanner had spoken with us

individually about their concerns and hopes, then maybe things would be different. Pregnant or not, it is time I return to the U.S. and complete what Betsy and Johnny had requested of me.

As soon as we are seated, Missy says, "Damn, Essy. You still have it. Adrian would never dare stand in your way again."

Essy shakes her head. "Missy, there is a time and place for everything. Of course, every woman has the right to protect herself. But there is a time and place where a large bulking male comes in handy."

"Yeah, yeah. Adrian has to realize I can take care of myself." Missy glances out the window and then turns back to Essy. "What I don't get. Why did Adrian suddenly back down?"

Essy and I both giggle and smile. "Maybe because you are with a trained bodyguard who knows how to do her job!"

Missy frowns. "Are you kidding me right now?"

Both Essy and I shake our heads. "No. That would be why he backed off."

Missy crosses her arms over her chest and lets out a huff.

"Men!"

Once we hit U.S. soil and with Essy at my side, we collect everything Johnny requested. With trust an issue, we made copies of the paperwork and documents, and made sure Neil looks over the legal documents. On our fourth day, we met up with Missy.

"How's everything going?" Missy states as she sits beside me in the back of Tanner's limo.

"We met with our father yesterday. He couldn't believe the evidence we uncovered. He's been in meetings ever since."

"Seriously? That quick?"

"Yes. He wanted to get the ball rolling. Tonight, he's organizing several strike teams from his trusted contacts."

"I'm amazed he didn't have you joining them, Essy."

"Hah. He would have until he had word that I'm pregnant!"

"Declyn," Missy states.

Essy nods. "Dad had mentioned that since we left to go to Australia, certain government departments have had major shake-ups. Unearthing and discovering spies and double agents against the U.S."

Missy shakes her head in disbelief. "No wonder the U.S. is in such a state."

All I do is nod in agreement.

The limo pulls along the curb in front of the New York high-rise building containing Missy's advertising business. We exit the car, dodge several fast-paced people on the sidewalk, and enter the busy ground floor via the spinning entry door.

A long floor runner leads to the elevators to prevent people from sliding and slipping along the floor. A face I remember behind the information desk smiles and waves at us. We wave back to Franklin and smile.

As soon as we step into the elevator, a tall, handsome stranger follows us in. Before the doors begin to close, the sensation of dread fills me.

I glance at Essy and nod as we both raise our brows. From the look on her face, she has tingles. Her own warning sensations have never failed her.

She quickly glances at Missy and then at me. I nod and casually say, "Missy, your top is doing that thing again. Here, let me fix it."

Sensing something wrong with my words, Missy moves enough as I step toward her.

From the corner of my eye, I notice something in the stranger's hand as I reach out for Missy and murmur, "Rainbow." Essy takes the hint, moving quickly. She steps around me with such force she grabs and pins the tall stranger to the elevator wall before he can contemplate what is happening. At the same time, she wraps her fingers around his right wrist and thrusts his hand towards his leg.

He releases a grunt of pain. Then his legs give out.

Essy allows him to hit the floor of the elevator on his knees.

She kicks his hand to remove a syringe from his fingers.

One of her hands quickly brushes over him, checking his pockets and discovering a handgun and two other syringes filled with an unknown liquid, and passes them to me.

She then moves his hands behind his back.

"Lady, release me at once," he slurs.

Missy reaches for her cell and makes a call. "Gayle, hello. I require your service at my office ASAP. Yes, I'm on the thirtieth floor. An unknown man attacked us. Yes, he has a gun... ...You remember Essy? She has apprehended him. ...Thank you, I'll let her know. See you shortly."

Missy smiles and glances at Essy. "A friend down at the New York PD recommends we entertain the man in any way we see fit. She suggests restraining him until she arrives with her detective partner and several police officers."

The stranger grunts as Essy lifts his arm a little higher behind his back.

"Sounds like a plan to me."

The elevator dings on the thirtieth floor, and the doors open wide. I help Essy lift and urge the stranger from the elevator on heavy legs towards the seating area outside Missy's office. We place the stranger on a chair, and I head into the office with Missy. She walks into a room kept for stationary and other spare office equipment. In a tall cupboard to the right, Missy opens it and lifts out a box with odd costume party accessories. She reaches in, pulls out a couple of pairs of metal handcuffs, and smiles.

"I knew these would come in handy!" Missy laughs, walks back to Essy, and hands them to her. "Here. I think you would know how to use these."

Essy stares at Missy and then at the handcuffs. "Should I ask why you have these?"

Missy shakes her head with a smile. "No. Best not to." And walks back into her office.

Essy makes quick work with the handcuffs around the stranger's wrists at his back behind the chair. She then searches the rest of his pockets and retrieves his wallet, pulling out his driver's license.

"So, Mark Brownly. Why are you here? Who was your target?"

The stranger we now know as Mark glares at Essy. "I'm not telling you anything," he slurs.

I reach for my cell and text our father to inform him of the situation in the elevator.

"What's in the syringe?"

He slowly shakes his head. "No-t…t…tel-ling," he mumbles

"What are you hiding?"

His eyes lose focus, and he slowly moves his head from side to side. Then, before he can stutter another word, his unfocused eyes roll up as his body leans to the side as he passes out. His cuffed arms were the only thing keeping him on the chair.

"Well, that is interesting," Essy murmurs. Then, with a frown, she turns and stares at the syringes on the desk. "Who sent him? And what was in those syringes?"

"That is the million-dollar question. But what was his agenda?"

My cell vibrates in my hand. I glance down to see my father's name on the screen.

"Dad's calling."

Chapter Fifty-Two

LAINI

After yesterday's fiasco, we reschedule our meeting with Francine.

My father places his other investigation on hold, arriving early this morning to investigate and confront the stranger, Mark Brownly. No one messes with his girls!

A WEEK LATER

"Daddy, thank you. Betsy and Johnny can now rest in peace." Thanks to my father, he contacted a special ops team to assist in the takedown of the Apolo Syndicate. What they did still astounds me. Five minutes ago, Daddy arrived at my hotel to update me on the latest news.

"It has taken a few favors to be called in. But everything worked out. Now we can officially say the Apolo Syndicate is over. We never have to think about them ever again." If only it is true. Time will tell.

"It's a bit hard not to, Dad. Mother was part of them."

"Laini love, your mother was used by that horrible family. She had thought Pedro was her father. He used her, mentally and physically abusing her. When I discovered he was the one responsible for my son's death. I wanted to bring Pedro back from the dead and kill him painfully and slowly. What he did was unforgivable. What kind of animal destroys the life of a baby?"

"It broke my heart when I discovered what the despicable man did to you both. Mother thought she had her father's love. Everything she had done was for that man's approval and love."

"What are your plans for today, pumpkin?"

With everything going on, I have not heard my father say that name in a long time. "Essy and I have an important meeting with Missy, which we have postponed long enough."

"Anything I should be made aware of?"

I give my father a look of innocence, wondering if he knows what is going on. "No. But Essy and I will need to speak with you soon, though."

"Should I be concerned?"

"Daddy, once we know the full details, we'll let you know." My father gives me his *you're hiding something* look. He shakes his head, then smiles.

"How are you and Essy feeling? Are you both coping with your morning sickness?"

We are not happy with our husbands. They had to blab to our father that we were pregnant. To tell you the truth, Essy and I saw our OB yesterday. We had several tests, including blood taken, and we both had an ultrasound. At least we know our pregnancies are progressing as they should, and this time I am already taking women's pregnancy multivitamins. As for our husbands — this is one time they missed out on seeing their child. Maybe next time, the men should discuss specific topics with us.

"I have good and bad moments. Providing I do not rush or smell a variety of coffee flavors, meats, or eggs, I'm fine."

"Sounds fun. When are you going to speak with your husband?"

My shoulders slump at his words, and I release a sigh. "Dad, do not push it. We are still annoyed with the boys."

"Laini, don't make Jax wait too long. He should be there for you this time."

"As I said, Dad. Don't push it. Even though I miss him and the kids… I'll phone them tonight."

"Good to hear. Now give me a hug. I have to go."

My father and I hug and say our goodbyes. I watch him walk out the door and think of the turmoil he must be going through. Essy and I hope he will discuss Mom with us. He might have been undercover, but he still loved her in his own way.

I look at my watch. It was nearly time to leave and meet Essy, Missy, and Neil for our meeting with Francine.

Once again, Essy and I step out of a town car and ride the elevator to the thirtieth floor, where Missy is waiting for us.

"Does Francine suspect anything?" I ask Missy.

She shakes her head. "No. She thinks we're here for a meeting to advertise Essy's business."

I nod. Good.

This is one of those moments you do not know how it will work out. I just hope Francine has an open mind.

Entering Missy's thirtieth-floor office, I'm not sure what to expect.

Neil walks out of his office with his bubbly personality and briefcase.

"Hello, ladies. It is fabulous to see you back in the New York office," Neil purrs with his trademark smile. "Pity your husbands are not here. I always enjoy a bit of testosterone at any time of the day," he flirts. The cheeky man has had a thing for our husbands. His smile then disappears, and just like that, Neil turns from his friendly, playful self into his business persona. "Now, we better get down to business before our meeting with Francine. Princess, lead the way. Everything is set."

Neil is one handsome male specimen. Even though I'm married, I'm not blind. Neil still turns heads wherever he goes, both male and female. He could have been a high-fashion model. He has the looks, body, and attitude. But, he preferred law and advertising.

We walk into Missy's office. "Righto, ladies. I have relooked over all the documents. What was required to be submitted and lodged has been. Everything is in place." Neil turns back to me. "Laini, I understand you have the photo albums."

I nod. "Yes. There are three of them. I'll place them on the table when Francine is seated."

"Good. What about Francine's parents? Did they agree to reveal the truth?"

Missy sits behind her desk, Essy to her left, Neil to her right, and I in one of the two armchairs opposite her. Nancy, the main receptionist, brings in our hot beverages and a platter of mixed cookies.

Once the door is closed again, I answer Neil, "Yes. Thankfully, they were relieved for the truth to be revealed. They had wanted Francine to know for several years, but Johnny said no." I glance at my watch. "Mr. and Mrs. Burton should be on their way here."

We continue to discuss Betsy and Johnny's lives. After discovering what the couple went through behind closed doors with the Apolo Syndicate, it is amazing that Johnny and Betsy survived as long as they did.

Several minutes later, Nancy was buzzing through to Missy to inform her that Francine's parents had arrived.

"Thanks, Nancy. Walk the Burtons to the conference room. When Francine arrives, wait five minutes, then buzz her. Let her know she is required in my meeting."

"Sure thing, Boss. Should I bring in fresh tea and coffee to the conference room?"

"Yes, please."

LAINI

"Thank you. For many years, we have wanted Francine to know the truth. Johnny had refused, saying it was unsafe for her to know."

"With the Syndicate now dismantled, and all the hidden assets uncovered, hopefully, this will be the end."

"Yes. We all deserve to live safely without keeping an eye over our shoulders," Mrs. Burton says.

We shake their hands in farewell and smile.

"Francine, if you have any other questions, don't hesitate to contact me," I say.

With the photo albums clutched in her arms, she nods, then turns for the door with Missy by her side.

Francine was not impressed to discover her parents in the conference room waiting for her to arrive. She felt ganged up on and lied to. On the other hand, at least several of her questions had been answered. She has a lot to think about with all the new facts regarding her family background.

The conference door closes behind Missy, Francine, and her adoptive parents.

All I can think is, *wow*.

My sister stands and paces to the large window overlooking the street. "Francine had taken the news about her birth parents and her mafia family background extremely well," Essy says over her shoulder.

I nod. At one point, I had thought we had pushed Francine too far. But then, at other times, I couldn't determine if she genuinely believed us.

"I think it helped to have her parents here and have them confirm the contents of the photographs."

"Yes. Thankfully, we arranged for them to arrive today. Without them, I think Francine would have phoned the police."

I nearly laughed at the woman when she did say that, including an ambulance, to have us committed.

Mind you, at times, I wonder.

"I was a little surprised when Francine mentioned how she had previously met Johnny. She wondered if he might have been a relation of some kind. Now she knows the truth."

Once I revealed how I met Johnny and what he wanted me to do on his behalf, Francine was nearly ready to walk out the door in disbelief. Thankfully, Betsy and Johnny had mentioned a few personal details to help me make Francine believe me. It worked, thankfully.

Francine now has to decide if she will continue working at the advertising agency or retire, as she is now a very wealthy woman thanks to Betsy and Johnny's investments and the family money.

"Laini, I have a meeting with our brother in a week. Tomorrow he will undertake his physical, including blood work."

"Will you be testing his DNA?"

"Yes. We have to be sure he is our brother."

I nod. "Essy... have you seen a picture of him?"

She shakes her head. "No." I don't know whether to take that as good or not.

We need to know if this stranger is our biological brother or not.

Chapter Fifty-Four

LAINI

With everything going on and finally my busy schedule is nearly complete. I have one more meeting with my agent this afternoon. Then I'll be meeting up with my kids for an early dinner at our favorite Italian restaurant.

Tanner had arranged to fly the boys, our kids, and the last of the employees back here to the States now the Apolo Syndicate was gone.

Missy, Essy, and I are still holding a grudge against our husbands. We are continuing to make them feel bad for how they handled the surprise pregnancy stuff.

The jury is still out on whether the boys had somehow planned for Missy, Essy, and myself to fall pregnant.

After serious discussions with one another, the three of us decided we would continue the pregnancies together. Discovering none of us are carrying twins — a relief. However, I still have bad bouts of morning sickness, and I'm looking forward to the day it stops.

Just as I am about to step out of the elevator for my one p.m. meeting, my cell begins to vibrate. Not wanting any interruptions, I allow it to go to the message bank.

As I sit in the reception waiting area, my cell vibrates again.

Who in the world is phoning me?

Chapter Fifty-Five

JAXTON

hy isn't my wife answering her cell?

If I'm not careful, panic will set in, and I'll have an anxiety attack.

Her father assured me we were safe. The Apolo syndicate is completely shut down and will never annoy us again. My ex-wife told me our parents were overwhelmed by the news regarding the Apolo Syndicate. I reminded her for me to be kept out of their lives. No way in hell do I want to be mixed in any more mafia family drama.

I had hoped to end all ties with my parents and what they had done to me all those years ago.

I missed so much with Laini and my daughter. Then the mafia was back in our lives, and both Laini and I nearly died. No. No more mafia connections.

Come on, Laini, answer your cell.

Many thoughts race through my mind.

Are you safe? Why aren't you answering your cell, Laini?

My cells stop ringing, and I hear my gorgeous wife's voice.

"Jax. I'm about to step into a meeting. I'll call you back afterward."

My heart breaks, and I feel lost after Laini left to return to the States. Damn Tanner and Dekk for convincing me to go along with them regarding the pregnancy surprise.

"Laini, wait."

"Jax, I have to go. My agent is calling me in."

"Laini, can we meet before you have dinner with the kids?"

"Why, Jax? Look, I have to go. Bye."

Before I can say another word, the line goes dead.

Damn it.

I want my wife. I miss her. It will break my heart if she decides she doesn't want to go ahead with the pregnancy. But I want my wife back. I want my family back as one.

"Was that Laini?" Tanner asks from beside me.

I nod. "Yes. She is still refusing to see me. I wish I didn't agree to go along with you and Dekk. I want my wife back."

"Look, Jax. I agree. Our wives have kept us all at arm's length for long enough. It is time for them to see reason."

"No offense, Tanner. For an ex-Dom who is used to wrapping women around your little finger, I bet Missy is still refusing to speak with you."

"Yes, well. My wife is her own person. A person I

love. I must convince her to allow me back into her life."

I snort at his words. Tanner, of all people, should have known better.

"Tanner, if Missy allows you to go anywhere near her again, I would expect her to demand you to get the snip."

"Yeah. That thought had crossed my mind. I'm booked in next week for the procedure." Oh, boy. I bet Tanner has not thought this through. "Never again. I want my wife to be unexpectedly pregnant."

"Um, Tanner. Have you mentioned any of this to your wife?"

He shakes his head. "Why?"

"Oh, Tanner. This is serious. For your own marriage, you better speak with your wife first."

"What... You really think so?"

"Yes. Don't be a fool and get the snip without speaking with your wife. And make sure you choose your words carefully when you talk with Missy. Or you might find yourself kept on the outer for a long time."

He nods and shakes my hand. "Thanks for the advice, Jax."

Chapter Fifty-Six

LAINI

What am I going to do regarding my husband?

I miss him.

But he hurt me.

My moods, anger, and feelings have exploded. I never act or feel this way. What is wrong with me?

"Laini, are you listening to me?"

Huh. What?

I glance toward the beautiful brunette opposite me and realize I am in the middle of a meeting with my agent. "Sorry, Marge. I was deep in thought."

"It looks like you are having man troubles. Am I right?"

I nod. "Yes. My husband hurt me."

"He what? Do I need to hurt him?" She slides her chair back, ready to hunt my husband down. The woman is only five foot four.

I throw my head back and laugh. "No. No, Marge. Jax stuffed up. Instead of discussing a delicate matter with me, he agreed to go along with two other men. Big mistake. Three wives are no longer speaking with their husbands."

"I wouldn't like to be in their shoes, then."

"No. You wouldn't."

"As I was saying before. I love your manuscripts. There are a few changes to be made. Other than that. I think you have another best seller on your hands. Well done. I cannot wait to see the completed books."

Relief fills me. "Thanks, Marge. I'm pleased to hear that. When do you require the updated manuscripts?"

"I can allow a month, but no longer. Do you think they will both be complete by then?"

I shrug. "Time will tell."

Marge knows not to push me. She knows I am not in the writing industry for the money. I've said to her once before I wouldn't mind dipping my toes into the indie publishing area. No deadlines. I can go by my own time frame.

I stand and shake Marge's outstretched hand.

"Thanks for seeing me, Marge."

"Always. Don't be a stranger. Keep in touch."

With that, I turn and walk out.

Time to phone my husband. We have a lot to discuss. But, with mixed emotions and thoughts, I think I have made him wait long enough.

Chapter Fifty-Seven

JAXTON

ith Emma's assistance, we prepare Jack for the kids Italian dinner with their mothers. Us husbands are not invited. Only to prove we are still on our wives' shit list.

I don't know how much more I can take from being separated from Laini. Each day breaks my heart a little bit more without being with her. Another day I missed out on our pregnancy.

Just as Emma picks up her baby brother, my cell rings. We both glance towards the screen. Emma smiles when she notices her mother's picture.

"I'll leave you to speak with Momma in peace while I feed Jack his bottle."

I nod and smile. "Thanks, Emma. Wish me luck."

She shakes her head and walks out of the bathroom. "You're on your own, Dad." And laughs at my predicament.

As quickly as I can, I pick up and swipe the screen of my cell.

"Laini. Thank you for calling back."

"Jax, we need to talk."

Oh, no. Whenever a woman says that it is not a good sign.

"Laini, is everything okay?"

"As I said, Jax. It is time we spoke. Let Emma know. I'll be over soon."

"You're coming over here?"

"Yes, Jax. Do you have a problem with that?"

Shaking my head, I reply, "No. No. I'll let Em know. She's feeding Jack his bottle. ...Before you say anything. Emma saw your name on my cell and wanted to give us some privacy."

"You don't have to explain, Jax."

"I didn't want you to get the wrong idea."

"I'll see you all soon."

Before I can say goodbye, Laini has already ended the call.

As I said. That is not a good sign.

I walk from the bathroom and straight to Emma and Jack.

Emma smiles as soon as she sees me. "How did the call go?"

"Em, your mother is on her way here. She wants to speak with me."

Her smile turns into a frown. "Dad, what are you not saying?"

"That is just it, Emma. I don't know."

A knock sounds on the door.

My pulse races to the sound, hoping Laini is here.

I reach for the handle and open the door.

There, standing in all her glory is my beautiful wife. My fingers twitch. All I want to do is reach forward, grab the annoying woman, and wrap my arms around her.

"Come in, Laini."

"Momma, come in," our daughter says from behind me.

Laini steps into our room and smiles at Emma, and reaches for Jack.

"Here. Let me hold Jack."

"Momma, Jacky is ready for bed. If you allow me, I'll place him down so you can speak with Daddy."

"No, rush, Emma. I would like to hold your brother, and I'll lay him down when I'm ready." Emma frowns and passes Jack to her mother. "You might as well continue getting ready, Emma. Aunt Essy will be here in twenty minutes to pick you up."

"What do you mean?" Emma shakes her head. "What are you doing, Momma? Why are you acting this way?" Yes, I would like to know as well. What is going through my wife's head?

"Emma, tonight you will stay with your aunt and

cousins. Your father and I have a lot to discuss and work out."

"What is there to work out? We're a family. We belong together. We need to go home together," she demands.

"Emma, it is not that easy. Your father broke my trust."

Our daughter shakes her head. "So, he can apologize and say sorry. Whatever he did, he will not repeat it." Emma looks at me with pleading eyes. "Will you, Daddy? You will not break Momma's trust again, will you?"

"Emma. Go and get ready and pack your toothbrush."

"What about Jacky?"

"Jack will remain here with your father and me."

Emma shakes her head and storms off to the room she has been sharing with Jack.

The baby continues to sleep against my wife's shoulder. I cannot believe I am jealous of my son. The lucky kid, at least one of us, can enjoy being in her arms.

"Come. Sit down, Laini. Would you like a drink? Tea, water... maybe coffee?"

"Water will be fine, thanks," she replies and gulps. But, if I am not mistaken, just mentioning the word coffee has her turning a little green. Interesting!

I grab two bottles of water from the minibar. I unscrew the cap and pass the bottle to her.

"Thank you," Laini says with a smile and takes a small sip.

"How have you been?" I ask. "Are you well?" She raises her brow at me in response.

"Jax, you hurt me. You broke my trust. You lied."

Huh? Now, wait a minute. I never lied to her.

"I have not lied to you, Laini."

"Haven't you?" She wiggles to the edge of her seat and stands. "Once Emma has left, we will continue this conversation." She then places her lips against Jack's head and turns her back to me.

Chapter Fifty-Eight

LAINI

*W*hat am I doing?

The whole situation has gotten out of hand.

The last thing I wanted to do was make Jax or my daughter angry. Emma left five minutes ago with Essy, and here I am, still holding onto my son as a lifeline. Time to speak with Jax.

I carefully place Jack in his crib, covering him with his little blanket. Then, I proceed back to the main living area and reach for my bottle of water, which I left on the floor beside my seat.

"Laini, now that our daughter has left for the evening, you are going to explain to me what you meant by me lying to you."

Now for the uncomfortable part.

"Jax, in all the years I have known you, never once had you mentioned your family was in the mafia."

I observe his face, and sure enough, he flinches.

"Laini, please understand. Growing up, my parents

had hidden their mafia family and connections from me. It was not until I was forced into marrying my ex-wife that the truth was revealed. By then, I was employed by the FBI, and my true identity was used against me."

"Jax, you could have said something to me."

"How, Laini? If the FBI had known the truth... back then."

"Don't you understand, Jax? They had known. The FBI and CIA had always known. They kept a close eye on you to see if you would betray them."

"But, I never did. I had been faithful to the government. I worked my butt off for my country."

"Yes, you had. That is another reason my father never shot you."

"What are you saying?"

"I'm saying my father had known about you. He had known my mother's connections to the Apolo Syndicate. He was not the only one — so had several other government officials."

"Why are we discussing this now?"

"Why? Because, Jax, I want no secrets between us."

"Laini, why do I feel there is something you haven't mentioned?"

"Because I have been a secret government agent working alongside Essy when I was required."

"You?" he says in disbelief. My nostrils flare. How dare he think so low of me.

"Yes. Me." So, my husband does not believe in my ability to be an agent. So much faith — not. "And if I choose to, I can work alongside the FBI and CIA." His facial features change when he realizes I am serious. "Only I work on my terms."

He frowns as if he thought of something. "I never understood why you didn't join the program as Essy had."

"Because I wanted to do something else with my life." I preferred fiction to non-fiction in my life. The reason I became a writer. "I thought having three other family members as government agents was enough."

"But didn't you just say you became one, anyway?"

"With my skills and talent — I was useful. You should have known my test scores were nearly a match for Essy's."

"I still don't understand?"

"And Jax. You never will. And that is all I can say."

"Okay, with being honest — I wanted you to know — I had no idea you could conceive again so soon after we had baby Jack. I stupidly went along with Tanner and Dekk, as they thought they knew the right way to handle the suspicion of you three being pregnant at the same time."

"As you know, that was the stupidest thing you could have ever done."

"Yes. I know that now." He sits down beside me. "Laini, it is destroying me to be away from you. Not able to touch you, hold you. The kids miss you. I miss you."

"Jax, why would me being away be any different from any other time when I'm on business, or you, for that matter?"

Jax stands and paces towards the window, shaking his head. "Are you serious right now?" he says over his shoulder. "It is different because you made it different, Laini."

I stand and move directly behind Jax.

I'm a writer for a living, and yet the right words are not leaving my mouth.

My focus is on the floor-to-ceiling window, watching Jax's reflection. I can see he is looking outside but not focusing on anything.

He shakes his head. "Laini, we agree to disagree." He turns, meeting my eyes. "You are my love, my soul mate." He turns to the window again. "But, if we cannot get past this, I don't know if we can continue."

Whoa. Well, color me rainbow colors and tie my hair in ribbons. I didn't see that one coming.

Chapter Fifty-Nine

JAXTON

ow. I can't believe I just said that. But, on the other hand. I cannot take it anymore.

All I want is my wife, and all she seems to do is push me further away.

Damn Tanner and Dekk. If only I didn't listen to them. I wonder if they are speaking with their wives yet?

"Jax, please listen to me. I love you. The last thing I want is to end our marriage. We have been through so much. We cannot allow it to end like this."

Huh?

"Why are you making things difficult? You said I lied to you. You keep repeating I broke your trust. How many times do I have to apologize for going along with Tanner and Dekk? I just want my wife and family back together."

I watch Laini's eyes mist up and her lower lip tremble. Oh, no. Now I've made my wife cry.

Maybe what Tanner and Dekk said to me yesterday

is true. A pregnant woman's hormones are confusing and deadly.

I wrap my arms around her, and she hiccups and then snuggles into my chest. I breathe her in and close my eyes. She feels like heaven within my arms, and savor the moment.

"Jax, I don't know what is wrong with me." Huh? My eyelids snap open. "Why am I so mean? This is not me."

My arms tighten around her. "Maybe your pregnancy hormones are to blame?" I whisper.

Laini pauses and lifts her tear-streaked face. "Do you think so?"

"Maybe? You are one of the nicest, most thoughtful, and loving people I know."

"Oh, Jax. I hope you are right. I don't want to be the bad guy. I never want to act like this. I love you, Emma and Jack."

That is it. It's time to take advantage of an empty suite before our little guy, Jack, wakes. I need to hold my wife and show her what she means to me. How much I love her.

As carefully as possible, I lift her in my arms and carry her to my room, gently placing her on the bed. I join her and wrap my arms around her holding her tight.

My arm is stiff and numb. Why is it failing to move? A familiar scent fills my nostrils, and a smile forms.

My wife.

I open my eyes and glance down my front. There, in all her sleeping beauty plaster against me, is Laini. Wondering what the time is, I turn my head the other way to glance at the bedside clock.

It is late. Much later than I would have imagined with a baby sleeping in the next room.

Strange. It is quiet. Too quiet.

As carefully as I can, I manage to slide my arm out from under Laini and stand without waking her. Then, once my brain kicks in, I shuffle to the next room and check on my son.

In the dim light, I can just make out my little man's gorgeous eyes staring right back at me. I'm amazed he is so quiet. Usually, he is loud and demands his bottle ASAP.

"Heya, little man. Are you hungry?" I reach down and pick him up, placing him against my chest. "First things first. Fresh diaper, then bottle. How does that sound?"

Jacky squeals his baby gurgles and pats my chest. Okay. I get it I must move faster. It does not take us long to replace his diaper and change it into a clean onesie and walk back to the kitchenette to heat his bottle.

Sitting down on the comfortable lounge with my back resting against the cushions, Jack gulps his bottle and snuggles into my chest as I gently rub his back.

"Come on, little man. I want to go back to bed," I mumble.

My little boy's response is rubbing his face against me while his little hand taps against my chest. Yep. My boy is tired. The little bugger is fighting the urge to go back to sleep.

Chapter Sixty

LAINI

My mind fills with annoying thoughts.

What in the world is wrong with me?

My attitude. Behavior. These stupid tears.

Why am I sprouting such hurtful words?

My nose presses into the soft pillow under my head. The delicious scent of my husband fills my nostrils.

Hang on a minute... why is my head against a pillow smelling of my husband? The last I remember, Jax and I were speaking in his hotel suite. Come to think of it, we were arguing to the point I could not believe what I was saying. First, pushing my daughter away, then my husband. Then, the way I spoke to my daughter...I was so harsh. I'm never snappy with her.

I have to do something to make things better. I want my family back. What did Jax say... something about pregnancy hormones? I sure hope that is what is causing me to be mean.

Everything has built up inside my head since

waking from the coma. I feel confused, agitated, and annoyed, just to name a few. Did I say annoyed? Essy mentioned I seem to be displaying a mixture of symptoms ranging from Anxiety, PTSD, and maybe depression.

Most likely caused by all the trauma since my childhood. The mafia has a lot to answer for, killing my birth parents. Which lead to me going into protective custody, then everything that has since happened. It has affected me in ways I could never comprehend. Not once have I had therapy.

I better text Essy. With the tornado of mixed emotions spinning out of control inside me, it is best for me to seek help. The last thing I want is to lose my family.

A smile fills my face when I notice my handbag beside the bed in the dim lighting. I reach for it and slip my cell free.

It does not take me long to tap out a message to Essy.

ME:

> Hey. Can you set up an appointment regarding what we were discussing? It's time. Thank you. L

Three dots appear, informing me she's reading my message. Followed by a ding.

ESSY:

> All done! The appointment is tomorrow at 1.30 p.m.. Are you OKAY?

My lips twitch at the corners, then I frown. I have the feeling my sister had already made the appointment. Thank goodness she is there for me. I love her so much.

ME:

Not sure. I need help to sort out my shit. I fell asleep, and Jax placed me in his bed. About to go looking for him.

ME

How's Emma? I treated her badly. I feel awful.

ESSY:

Don't worry about it. I was honest with her. She had noticed you seemed different since you woke from the coma and was concerned.

My poor daughter. Why hasn't she said anything to me? I have to make myself better for me. I have to be there for my family.

ME:

Thank you. Can you let her know that I love her?

ESSY:

Already did. She had also asked if it was a result from you being in a coma.

ME:

I have an intelligent daughter. Jax is not back yet. I better find him.

ESSY:

Yes. Go and have some special
bonding time. LOL

Typical Essy. Thinking of sex. Then it occurs to me.
Eww. What have I interrupted?

ME

What about you and Dekk?

ESSY:

Let me just say, he is being extra nice
to me.

Eww. Too much information.

ME:

Why do I have the feeling the kids are
all asleep!

ESSY:

Because they are. LOL

ME:

Okay. I'm going now. Luv Ya.

ESSY:

Luv u 2

From the bed, I quickly use the bathroom and
freshen up, then search to see where my husband has
disappeared. Come to think of it. My son has been
quiet. Maybe Jax is feeding Jack his bottle.

*A*s soon as I step through the bedroom door towards the flickering light coming from the wall television in the main living area. My focus goes straight to the lounge. The first thing I see is the top of a head at one end and a bare foot at the other. With each step closer to the lounge, more of my husband appears. My lips twitch at the sight. Spread out along the lounge, with his arms wrapped securely around our son. My heart fills with love. How I have missed the two special men in my life.

I step toward them and carefully remove Jack from Jax's chest. My husband stirs a little and goes back to sleep. My son snuggles into me and grabs a handful of my blouse. I press my lips to his head and close my eyes as his baby scent fills my nostrils.

I slowly walk to the room with the baby crib, and as careful as I can be, I gently unhook his fingers from my top and place him in his bed, covering him with his blanket.

"Sleep tight, my little man. I love you."

I stand there looking down for several seconds, memorizing my son's innocence.

Right. Time to speak with Jax.

I rub my heated core against him — the kiss increases in intensity.

Wow. What a kiss. If I were wearing socks, they would have blown off my feet. As it was, the intensity of our love-fueled kiss began to short-circuit my brain.

The room spins. Dim lighting fills my vision as Jax places me down on his bed, reaches for my clothing, and begins removing them piece by piece, followed by a kiss in each bared spot. Once he has me naked, he removes the last of his own clothing before joining me, crawling up between my spread thighs and placing more kisses along my flesh until he's leaning over me.

My gaze roves over his taunt, ripped body. Lingering a little longer on his scrumptious cock, its round mushroom-shaped weeping tip pointing straight at me. Hard, thick, and long. Very long and all mine. I slowly lick my lips with vivid thoughts of what I want to do with said cock.

The focus of my attention bobs up and down, cutting off my thoughts. I continue to admire my husband's body until my eyes meet his heated gaze with his trademark smile, informing me I must wait my turn and then I can do whatever I want with his dick.

"Now, my love. You asked me to take you to bed and make love to you," he says in a sexual husky voice. "And that is what I plan to do."

I nod and smile once more.

*O*ur heated flesh turns slick with sweat — the beat of our hearts races as one. Our souls sing, reconnecting and fusing together as our orgasms peak, and we soar above the clouds to the stars before slowly drifting back to earth in our bed, entwined within one another's arms.

My eyes remain shut. I'm too worn out to move my limbs.

"I love you so much, Laini. Please stay," Jax pleads.

My heart aches at his words, and a tear slips free.

"Jax, remember that I love you with all my heart."

"Why do I feel a but, coming on?"

Another tear slips free. I begin to frown, thinking of the right words to say. "Jax, I want to be me again. I know there is something wrong going on inside my head. Tomorrow I've got an appointment — the first of many. I require help. I need to know if you will still be there for me."

"Of course, I will be here. I'll remain at your side. Right, where I want to be. Never doubt my love for you, Laini."

I hiccup and wrap my arms around Jax tighter.

"Thank you, Jax."

"You don't need to thank me, Laini. You're my life. The mother of our children. The other half of my soul and heart. I love you more than all the stars in the galaxy. Always remember that when you doubt yourself."

I press my lips against his slick heated flesh, tasting his salted flavor.

"I love you more than the universe," I say with a smile. "Universe. Is bigger than the galaxy, right?"

Jax's laugh makes my grin turn into a full-blown smile.

"Oh, Laini. I'll stick with galaxy."

"Whichever way is bigger, you've had enough time to recover. Now husband, treat your wife right and show her how to travel to the galaxy so we can fly together forever!"

Jax snorts and busts out laughing before saying, "Don't I always, my love?"

I giggle and nod. With a cheeky smile, I reply, "There is always room for improvement."

"What the?" Jax moves between my thighs. Encasing me with his body. "I'll show you *room for improvement*!"

And he did. For the rest of the night until Jack woke for his next feed.

Chapter Sixty-Two

ESSY

With a cup of tea in my hand and several chocolate cookies on the plate. I wait patiently for my sister to sit down. She does with a sigh and then lifts her cup and takes a sip. She smiles and shrugs her shoulders.

"Sorry. I couldn't help it. It's the pregnancy. My bladder was protesting again."

My lips twitch. I know exactly what she is speaking of. I'm not about to inform her I went for the fifth time just before she arrived at my office. I'm glad Laini came early, though. Last week I'd arranged for her to meet me here today. We're meeting my new staff member — our biological brother. He thinks he is meeting his new boss to go over last-minute paperwork.

Thanks to our biological mother keeping him a secret, we knew nothing of his existence until she died. But we cannot blame him either. He still does not know we are family. He thinks our mother was only his godmother. Plus, we must tell him that she died just over a month ago. So, we're not sure how that will go down. But, then discovering your godmother is your actual biological mother...It was a shock to me when I found out. The woman who had adopted me was, in reality, my biological mother, who had her embryos stolen.

This will be the first time the three of us will meet and see one another in person. I have held off from looking at his picture. I'm still not sure if that was a good thing or bad not seeing his image. My mind has created different scenarios of his face, body shape, and hair coloring.

Now for our pre-discussion. As Laini now has regular sessions with her new therapist, who specializes in trauma and post-natal depression, and a few conditions.

My lips touch the rim of my cup. The steam tickles my nostrils. I carefully take a sip and then place the cup on my desk.

"No worries, sis. Enjoy your cup of tea before it goes cold."

She nods and takes a sip. "Are you going to say what the results were? Is he our brother?"

I nod. "Yes. Yes, he is. Our mother was correct." I frown, thinking about our mother. All the lies and all the cover-ups over the years. "Now, how have your sessions been going? Is the therapist...is he any good?"

I watch my sister smile and nod her head. At least, that is good news.

"Yes. Thank you for organizing the first appointment. I'm starting to feel better within myself, which Emma and Jax are ecstatic about."

"That is fantastic news. I'm glad to be able to help. What about you and Jax? How are things between you both?"

Laini smiles. The type of smile I have not seen her display in a long time. The kind of smile she has when she is thinking about her husband. "We're good. He came with me to one session to meet the therapist and was included in the actual session. So Jeremy got to see how Jax interacts with me. He also asked Jax his point of view on my behavior from before and after the coma. Things like that."

"Wow. That is good. Jax could join in. I know he felt a little funny with you seeing a male therapist. Personally, I think he was jealous."

Laini nods. "Yes. I noticed that before he attended my session yesterday. Now, he is more relaxed with me attending my appointments."

"Didn't you have one today?"

"Yes. I came straight from there to here. I think that is why my bladder was protesting. I didn't have the time to go before I arrived here."

At that moment, my bladder indicated I needed to empty it again. Seriously! Not again.

"Okay. I get the message. Now, speaking of bladders, I better go before everyone arrives." I stand from my chair. "Now finish your tea, and I'll have my assistant bring in fresh cups."

Laini pulls a face. Then wiggles in her chair. "I think I have to go again?"

I shake my head.

Seriously.

Pregnancy!

This pregnancy has been different from my other two. I've never had this type of inconvenience.

Laini and I discuss in detail what we should say, what we need to say, and the topics to avoid. I had also prepared a folder, which our mother had originally prepared, explaining what had happened from the beginning. After reading the letter, I was shocked to discover a few more family secrets. So I made a copy for Laini. I watch her facial features as she reads her copy.

Her lips move to a straight line as her eyes look up from the sheets of paper and meet mine with a shake of her head. "You have to be bloody kidding me. If she were not already dead, I would give the woman a piece of my mind," she declares.

I nod. Yes. I agree wholeheartedly. What our father ever saw in the woman, I do not know. Maybe he sensed the abuse she had gone through and wanted to protect her from the people who she thought were her "family. She was a lost soul. She wanted to please a man who she had loved. Even though she knew he was an evil, bad man who also abused her — mentally, emotionally, and physically.

Why would anyone stay in that environment? We'll never know the truth. Susanna had told that many lies. We don't know if she even knew what was fact and what was fiction.

*W*hen my assistant notifies me that my eleven o'clock appointment had arrived, Laini and I are on our feet, facing the door.

My assistant opens the door to allow Mr. Tarret James Browns into my office.

As soon as my eyes meet Tarret's, I first notice his familiar features, so much like our fathers from when he was the same age. His smile slips, and he frowns when he glances at Laini and then back to me.

I reach out and offer to shake his hand. He automatically encases mine within his. A firm, warm grip. A touch that feels so familiar and yet so different.

"Thank you, Mr. Browns, for attending our meeting today. I'm Essy Raiker. From the look on your face, you have some questions."

"Yes. How'd you know?"

"I know that look anywhere, Tarret," I say. "First, I want you to meet my sister, Laini Travelli."

He looks from me to Laini and back to me again.

"Sister? Why am I really here, Essy?" Glad to see he is more intelligent than he looks.

"Well, Tarret. We will begin with a hot beverage, and you'll likely end up drinking spirits. Now please take a seat, and my assistant will be in here shortly with tea or coffee."

"Tea with milk will be fine," Tarret automatically replies.

"That is good to hear," Laini mumbles.

Tarret turns and looks at Laini. "Why is that?"

Laini smiles and places her hand on her lower belly. "Because the smell of coffee makes me nauseous."

Chapter Sixty-Three

LAINI

I cannot believe it. The stranger resembles our father. Even with the DNA results proving he is our brother, his looks alone would have stated the facts otherwise.

"Tarret, we arranged this meeting today not just for your new position with this firm, which you earned all on your own. But, the other reason of a personal nature."

Tarret places his cup down. It doesn't take a genius to see the man is not comfortable and wants to leave. I glance at Essy.

"Tarret. We knew your godmother."

Tarret pauses and sits back in his chair. "What do you mean, knew, not know."

"The woman whom you knew as your godmother was our mother. Susanna and her husband, James Raiker, adopted both Laini and myself. Only to discover years later we were, in fact, their biological children."

"What has that got to do with me?"

"Let me explain. Their only fertility-aided pregnancy ended in miscarriage. They later discovered several of their stored embryos were stolen from the fertility clinic and tried to track them all down. The day Susanna died, she revealed we had a brother."

"Look, Ms. Raiker. I still don't know where I come into all this. The woman I knew as my godmother, her name was not Susanna. It was Bethany."

Before Tarret could pronounce the surname, I said it instead. "Western. Bethany Western." That was our mother's undercover name when she was working the case with our father."

Tarret looks at me. "What case?"

"Our parents worked for the FBI. They had been partnered to work undercover together as a couple who could not conceive," Essy blurts. So much for keeping that part under wraps for a little longer. "The fertility clinic was under investigation. The clinic would inform couples that their embryos hadn't survived and would then sell the healthy embryos, implanting them into other women. That is how the three of us were born."

"No. My parents..."

Before he can complete his sentence, I place the photos in front of him, including all the paperwork.

"Here. Take a look at the photos and paperwork. We'll leave you to it for a few minutes."

Taret shakes his head, then leans forward, grabs the items from the desk, and begins to glance at the items and scan several documents.

"*W*hat were you thinking, blurting everything out?"

"Laini, Tarret was set to bolt. He's military. He'll prefer to have all the facts, no matter how unbelievable they are."

"How long should we leave him in there?"

Essy glances toward her open office door. "We'll have another drink, then go in. He'll most likely have several questions."

Right on cue. Essy's assistant appears with two fresh cups of tea. I reach for mine. "Thank you, K."

She smiles and passes the other cup to Essy. "Is everything okay, Boss?"

"Yes, K. Mr. Browns has important paperwork to sort through. We thought we would give him some space."

"Okay. Let me know if you require anything else," K replies, smiling before returning to her desk.

I shake my head. "Several questions will be an understatement, Essy."

Essy takes another sip from her cup. "Laini, have you thought about the fact our brother, a man we never knew existed, is sitting in the other room? Did you see how much he resembles Daddy?"

"Yes. I couldn't believe it. But I think you'll find, Tarret is several inches taller."

"I agree. He is bigger than Dad all over. He even has

a couple of Dad's tels. The way he tilts his head in thought..." Essy stops speaking when the man in question appears in her doorway.

"You know I can hear you," he tilts his head toward the office, "in there."

Well, tie me in ribbons. "Sorry. It's just seeing you. It makes it all real."

"Yes. The reality of having a brother. We never expected..." Essy says.

"You better come back in here then," he said. "We have much to discuss."

I nod along with Essy and stand. Tarret steps out of the open doorway, allowing us back into her office.

Essy goes back to her seat behind her desk. I sit back in the seat I was in when I arrived.

Essy picks up her phone and buzzes K for more tea. Within minutes, K walks in with a tray of cups of tea and places it on Essy's desk. "Thank you, K. Please hold all calls. We are not to be interrupted."

"Very, well, Boss. I'll leave you to it."

"Thanks, K."

K closes the door behind her, leaving the three of us sitting and staring at one another.

Tarret begins speaking first in a take-charge manner. Silly man. He will soon learn that tactic does not work with either Essy or me. "Ladies, I'll begin with I had Essy investigated." I glance at Essy, and she smiles and shrugs at me. "I am Military, and I do have connections." Essy and I nod. He's not the only one.

"And what did you discover, Tarret?"

"That is just it. You have several sealed files in the high-up government areas. It had me intrigued."

"As you know, I'm ex-FBI. So a lot of my past is sealed."

"Yes. But it also indicates you are also, Military."

Essy smiles. "My. You have been doing your homework. Even our parents do not know my Military history."

"You said our parents are or were FBI. Where is our father, and what does he do?"

This time I answer. "Our father works on need-to-know bases with the FBI. He and our mother started a security business. Essy, as you know, started her own bodyguard business."

"Okay, what do you do then?"

"As for me. I was an editor and reporter for a fashion magazine. My husband and I are now retired. We have two children. Teenage girl and a baby boy."

Tarret pulls a face in confusion. "How can you be retired? You're our age."

"Look, Tarret. Both Essy and I invested money at an early age, and with Essy's skills, we played the Stockmarket. We were successful."

Tarret turns to Essy. "So, wouldn't that make you semi-retired?"

Essy nods. "It would, but I am not able to slow down as yet."

"Why do I feel you guys are leaving out a lot of information?"

I tilt my head back and laugh. "Oh, Tarret. If only

you knew the half of what goes on behind closed doors."

Essy adds, "I'm married to Declyn Bianchi. And before you say anything. We both have our own money. So no, I do not sponge off my husband."

"Wow. The Declyn Bianchi of the Bianchi industries and all the other branches of his business." He pauses, then looks back to Essy. "Didn't he have a twin?"

Essy nods. "Yes. Leo. He died several years ago now. I was there when his fiancé shot him."

"Wow. What about you, Laini? Who did you marry?"

"I have been in a relationship and finally married Jaxton Travelli, also, now ex-FBI."

"I sense there is a story to that."

"Yes. I met Jaxton when I was a teenager. At the age of seventeen, I discovered I was pregnant with my daughter Emma. Before I could inform Jaxton, his parents moved him interstate as they had an arranged marriage organized."

"Wow. But how did you get back together?"

"When my daughter had an appendix attack, the hospital contacted him. Why, you might be thinking? If anything ever happened to me, I had Jaxton's contact details on my daughter's file."

"Why am I sensing a lot more missing from your story?"

I nod. "Long story short. At seventeen, no one except our mother knew I was pregnant. As far as anyone knew, I was traveling. Backpacking Europe. Once my daughter was born, she was placed in the care of a couple who were paid to raise my daughter."

"Geez. What happened next?"

"I still had contact with Emma. I refused to abandon my child. It was my money that paid for my daughter's care. Around the time Essy had her twin boys, I made it known I had a daughter. Our father was shocked. Mother never said anything to him. As for Jaxton, he was already in the process of obtaining a divorce."

"Was he getting a divorce because of you and his daughter?"

I shake my head. "No. His ex-wife was in a relationship with someone else. Jaxton and Juliet never loved one another. They had separate lives. When Jaxton's father died, he was free to obtain his divorce."

Tarret turns to Essy. "So, is your story as exciting?"

Essy laughs and throws her head back. "Depends. Dekk was my client. At the end of our contract, Dekk asked me to marry him in a marriage of convenience. To prevent his parents from marrying him to someone he didn't like."

"Seriously?"

"Yes. A business transaction, my father-in-law, wanted to further his contacts and bank balance. Anyway. After our short honeymoon, I went on a secret mission and nearly died. Several months later, while I was recovering, I was informed I was pregnant. So I retired from the Military, and the FBI, to concentrate on myself and my bodyguard business."

"You were still working in all those areas and operating a business. You both don't do things by halves."

Essy and I both shake our heads. "No. Anyway, with

no communication from Declyn, I went hunting for him. He needed to know about the pregnancy. Instead, I found Leo. Declyn and I finally got back together, and we have two healthy sons and, a few years later, a gorgeous little girl, Bella."

"Wow. I'm an uncle to what...three nephews and two nieces."

"Yes," I said. "Now, Tarret. What is your story?"

arret picked his cup up and drained it. We eyed the way he calmed his breathing to prepare himself. Sadness fills his eyes. "As you know, I was recently in the Marines — an eleven-year vet. I had been married for six years with a daughter and a son. While I was deployed on a four-week mission at the start of last year, my wife Gloria, four-year-old daughter Samantha, and two-year-old son Mathew were killed in a car accident." No. How awful for Tarret. I reach over and place my hand on his to offer comfort. My eyes mist. How tragic. "I wasn't informed until I returned. My wife's parents had held the funeral without me. So I never got to say goodbye."

I glance at Essy. Her eyes, like mine, were full of tears. Damn these pregnancy hormones. "We are so sorry for your loss, Tarret." Essy frowns and then asks, "Tarret, you said last year?"

Tarret snaps his focus back to Essy. "Why? Do you know something?"

"I'm not sure." What is Essy thinking? Then it occurs to me. Surely not...? "Had someone with the surname Apolo ever contacted you?" I shake my head in disgust. Now, I know where Essy is leading with her questions. The evil Pedro.

Tarret shakes his head. Then pauses with a frown. "A strange man had contacted me. His name was hard to make out. It sounded like Pet. Petrol, maybe Pedro something."

Essy shakes her head and looks at me with eyes displaying what we both have realized. "I think the name you're looking for is Pedro Apolo. He was head of the Apolo Syndicate. Mafia. Our mother had thought he was her father. When he discovered she was not of his blood, he used her until the end. She had always believed he was her father."

Tarret shakes his head in confusion. "Why would he contact me?"

I reply with, "He must have discovered who you were. What he does, is to control you. If you don't, then he kills your family members. He did that to his own children to keep them in line."

Tarret's mouth literally opens as his eyes widen before they narrow.

Essy then asks, "When was this contact with Pedro?"

"Before I was deployed on that mission when my family died." He glances at Essy, then at me, then back at Essy. "Are you saying if I had agreed to meet with that sicko, my wife and kids might be alive today?"

"Maybe. Maybe not. When it came to Pedro, he did

things to suit himself. I had witnessed him remove his own grandson's finger because the kid failed to follow instructions," I murmur. Seeing the vision flash through my mind.

"Geezus, christy. Are you serious?"

"Yes. Yes, I am." I give myself a mental shake to vanish the images.

"Where is this animal?" he demands.

Essy replies, "Someone bet you to it. He received a bullet to the brain a month ago. He is dead. I made sure of it."

"Did you shoot him?" Tarret asks with a raised brow.

Essy shakes her head. "No. But it would have been a bit of stress relief if I had."

Okay...A change of topic is required.

I glance at Essy and see her again, giving Tarret a strange look. It's a look she does when she is trying to place information together or a face.

"Have we met before today?" Essy asks Tarret. "I'm sure I know you from somewhere."

Tarret smiles and then lifts his brow. "I was wondering if you remembered."

Essy frowns. I can see she is still searching her memory for an answer. "Remembered? So we have?"

"I was one of the team members when your body was dragged from the river."

Her eyes widen. Her facial features, for once, reveal she is reliving that experience. "JT. Is that you?"

He smiles and nods. "As soon as I saw you today, it clicked. We had met previously."

She smiles and rushes around her desk. Tears stream down her face as she wraps her arms around his solid form. "You're the one who saved my life."

Chapter Sixty-Five

ESSY

Thankfully, I had K cancel today's and tomorrow's appointments. I couldn't believe it. Jarret is JT. He had been on the team I was on. It was a mixture of FBI and Military members. I think we had spoken to one another a few times on a night mission. We'd been in full-night cammies, including face paint. The following day I was sent in undercover for over a month or more.

I had thought I had made it up, hearing his voice when I was rescued from the rushing water. Now I know it was real. He was the one who risked his life, pulling me free from the debris hidden in the water.

"I always wondered what had happened to you. But, all we were told, you had survived. I never saw or heard anything about you since. Not until today. Now, look. It turns out you are my biological sister. No wonder the urge to save you was strong."

"Thank you, Tarret. When you meet my husband, he will also thank you. He's very appreciative. You didn't just save my life but also my two sons. I was pregnant on that mission."

"Oh, wow."

I turn to Laini. She wipes her face again with a soggy tissue. Her happy tears continue to run. The smile on her face has not left her face. She gets up from her chair and wraps her arms around him. "Thank you, Tarret. For saving our sisters' life."

I smile. I am so happy we have one another. "Tarret, our sister here has saved my life a time or two."

Tarret's eyes widen. "Seriously?"

She nods. "Yeah. I've been with her a few times where my services were required. I know how to use a gun, which Essy taught me when we were teenagers."

All Tarret could say was, "Seriously?"

We both reply, "Yep. Seriously." Then Laini and I burst out laughing.

Jarret had taken a copy of all the information back to his hotel room, including a copy of our DNA test confirming he is indeed our biological brother, with a copy of our mother's DNA test results she had taken when Tarret was young. A copy of the test results that our parents had organized to confirm we were their biological daughters.

Later that evening, we picked up Jarret for a big

family dinner. He was a little overwhelmed when he met our husbands and all our kids.

All the children loved discovering they have an uncle. I can already see their minds ticking over. They all have plans. I hope Tarret does not give in to all their demands.

Everyone is laughing at the different jokes the older children keep telling.

Laini passes baby Jack to Jax, and he rests the baby against his shoulder. The kid is adorable.

"So, Tarret. Will you be moving into the Raiker family building?" Jaxton asks.

Tarret glances at both Laini and me with his brow raised.

I smile and reply, "Our parents converted an old factory building into an apartment complex for all of us to stay in. However, there is an apartment that has not been used. Our mother had been slowly doing it up. I'm not sure where she was up to with it. I bet it was for you."

"What about our father? What would he say about his lost son moving in?"

I sensed our father walking up behind me. Plus, Laini's eyes widened as she mouthed, *Daddy*. Also helped.

"That depends. When can you move in?" he announces.

Everyone stands.

Laini and I contacted our father and wanted to see him in person. Instead, we had to handle everything over the phone regarding the news about Tarret. Daddy was at first shocked, then angry, which is understandable. Mother had kept us all in the dark. I sent a copy of the DNA report I had organized and a copy of the selfie photo Laini had taken of the three of us.

Daddy had mentioned how he had come across a dossier on Tarret and wondered why Mother had it. Now he knows. It was about their son.

"Hello, Daddy. How are you?" Laini brightly says.

"Laini, calm down and sit. You too, Essy. I don't want either of you going into labor."

Tarret looks at both Laini and me with a raised eyebrow. I nod to say, yes, we're both pregnant.

Our father walks around to where Tarret is standing and offers his hand. "Hello, I'm James Raiker. I understand you're my son."

Tarret, a little shocked, nods his head. "Yes, Sir. I believe I am. It is a pleasure to meet you." They shake hands before our father wraps his arms around his son. They stand there for several minutes in one another's embrace. Tears run down my face. I glance at Lain, and she has matching happy tears.

We nod at one another and join our father and brother in a big family hug.

Chapter Sixty-Six

LAINI

sharp pain rips right through my lower body.

Holy shit. What was that? The next thing I know, the sensation of peeing myself — well, flooding the bed would be a better account.

I lift the covers and look down. Color me in rainbow colors and tie me in ribbons. My waters have just broken. I'm officially in labor.

I reach for my cell and activate it to see the time. Ah, bugger. It's three in the morning. This kid has timing!

I sit up, and before I can swing my legs to the side of the bed, another sharp, tightening pain takes hold, causing me to catch my breath. Oh, boy. I watch the clock on my cell and attempt to remember my breathing for labor pain from our classes.

How I have not missed this part of the birth. It's too late to back out now.

The contraction is only a couple of minutes from the last one, and lasting forty seconds. Okay. I can do this. Once the contraction settles, I shake the shit out of Jax.

How he didn't wake up from all the fluid or with my groans. I have no idea.

"Jax, wake up. Wake up now. It's time."

"Huh. Laini? Go back to sleep, babe."

Just as I begin to speak, another contraction starts. "Arhhh." I try panting. I try to focus on my breathing technique. But nothing is working. "Fark. Jaxton, this bloody hurts. Get your ass out of this bed right now. It's time to go to the hospital."

Jax bolts upright and turns his lamp on. He freezes when he sees the condition of the bed. "Oh, shit. Your waters have broken!"

With the pain still running rampant, I ground out, "No, shit, Sherlock. Get dressed. Call Daddy. Get Emma."

Jax nods and scrambles out of bed. He throws on his jeans and t-shirt and slips his feet into his shoes. He reaches for his cell and dials my father.

Another contract hits. Groaning is about the only thing I can do.

"Jason. Hello, Jason. It's time. We need you to come over. Laini is in labor. ...What? Essy's in labor? Oh, no. Oh, okay, that will be great. Emma can watch Jack until you all arrive."

Oh, boy. My sister is in labor... It must be that time of the year for giving birth. I wonder how Missy is?

Once the next contract ends, I send a group message to my sister and Missy — to let them know I'm in labor.

Next thing, my cell dings with an incoming group video call. I hit accept, and Missy and Essy take up most of the screen in two boxes.

My sister speaks first, "Hey, I'm in labor."

I nod, "I think I need a new mattress."

She laughs. "Same. What a mess. I think it's too late to back out of the birth process. These contractions are hard and fast."

I nod. I completely agree. "Tell me about it. They bloody hurt." I look at Missy and see she is pulling faces, then I look at Essy, and she begins pulling faces. "Missy, are you in labor too?"

She nods, and next, we hear her grunting and groaning. Essy also fills the speaker with her contraction sounds. Before I can say another word, another contraction hits me. My belly tightens. The pain rips through my front and back, and I scream.

Jax comes running back into our bedroom with Emma not far behind him. "Are you on your cell?" I nod.

"The girls are in labor as well," I ground out.

Emma sits beside me and begins to rub my back.

Once the contraction settles enough, I say, "Jax, I need you to take a look. I think the baby is crowning."

"What? No. You have to go the hospital."

I pass the cell to Emma. "Em, can you turn around so Dad can check?"

She nods and scrambles away from the bed. The sound of screaming can be heard from my cell.

I lay back down in the wet, and Jax takes a look. His eyes widen. "Holy shit. I can see the top of the baby's head. What do I do?"

Another contraction hits.

Emma's voice can be heard calling for an

ambulance. "Yes, my mother is having a baby. My father can see the head."

I look to Jax. "Jax, grab towels to place under me."

He nods, bolts to the bathroom, and rushes back with several towels. I roll to the side as Jax shoves several towels under me. "Help sit me up and move the pillows behind me."

He nods. Another contraction rips through me. The urge to push starts. It looks like this little one will be born here and delivered by their daddy.

So far, Jax and I have refused to know the sex of the baby. We wanted it to be a surprise.

I reach out to Emma. "My cell. Are Missy and Essy still there?"

Emma nods and holds my cell away from her.

"Emma, go check on your baby brother. Then, I need you to grab some baby towels to wrap your sibling in. Then, go and wait for the medics to arrive. Love you, baby girl." She smiles, nods, and bolts from the room.

Another contraction rips through me. I look to Jax. He is scared shitless. Great. Just what I need. Once the contraction slows, I say, "Jax, go and wash your hands. I need to push. You're going to be delivering your child."

He nods and gulps, then turns and takes off for the bathroom.

I lift my cell and look at the screen. "Hey, guys. How are you going?"

Essy answers first. "I need to push."

Missy follows. "So do I."

The sound of their grunts and groans fills my speaker.

"Are any of you at the hospital?"

Missy nods. "I am. Arrived thirty minutes or so ago. What about you?"

I shake my head. "No. Still in my bed at home."

Essy grunts again and starts making a weird noise. From the background, I can see she is in her bed as well. I see Dekk appear. He resembles Jax. He looks scared out of his wits.

"Hey, Dekk. Set Essy's phone up so we can stay connected." I turn to Jax. "Jax, place the cell over on the side table so I can keep in contact with the others."

"Okay, babe." He lifts the cell from my hand just as another contraction rips through me. The urge to push is massive. I cannot wait any longer.

I hear Jax speaking with Dekk and Tanner.

"Jax," I scream. "I need you. I have to push."

"Oh, shit. What the hell do I do?"

I begin bearing down. I reach for my ankles. The sounds I make are non-human. The pain is unreal. I want it to stop. I keep pushing. My fingers grip around my ankles tighter. My knees spread wider.

"Laini, the baby's head has crowned. I need you to stop. Remember you said I had to remind you that when the head crowns, you must stop pushing."

Oh, my gawd. How in the hell am I meant to stop the urge to push?

My breaths are coming short and fast. I look to the side of my cell and focus on Essy and Missy.

"Hey, Essy. You crowning yet?" I yell out. I see Dekk look at the cell, and he nods. "Get her to stop. She has to stretch, or she'll tear." Dekk says something, and Essy turns to the cell, her face red and sweaty.

"This is fucking painful."

"Yeah. I completely agree. Is your ambulance on its way?" She looks at Dekk, and he nods. Thank goodness.

I glance at Missy's square. I can see she is screaming and bearing down. I say Tanner has the cell on mute. For I am certain Missy is swearing her head off at her husband.

"Hey, Essy. It looks like Tanner is getting an earful."

She nods and smiles. "Yeah, I think Dekk knows how Tanner feels."

Tightening and pain catch my breath, warning me of another contraction.

"Essy, good luck. I..." I didn't get the chance to finish. My body was demanding to push, and I began to scream.

I look to Jax. He's scared but ecstatic all at the same time. His hands are between my thighs. On my next breath, I say, "Jax, as soon as the head pops out, ensure the cord is not wrapped around the baby's neck. If you can, wipe the baby's face and clear the nose and mouth."

"Okay, baby. I'm ready."

After that, I'm too busy bearing down to say or listen to anything.

My throat feels raw from all the grunting and screaming as I push. The pushing and bearing down are never-ending. I manage another quick, deep breath and push again. Then, all of a sudden, I feel the baby's head pop out. My eyes widen. Jax barely has time to reach for the head when a massive contraction strikes. I bear down as hard as I can, screaming at the top of my lungs. I look down between my legs and watch.

A strange sensation with a slithering feeling happens. First, I see my baby's head and shoulders appear as Jax lifts our baby. Then, I feel a peculiar sensation as if the baby has just kicked me as they slip free from my body.

Jax's eyes meet mine. His face is full of amazement and disbelief.

Emma rushes in, followed by the medics.

I look to the side and see Essy has just given birth. A baby is placed on her chest. I look to Missy. She, too, has just given birth.

The sound of a baby's cry fills the room.

Tears fill my eyes.

I turn back to look at Jax, then watch the medics open their bags and pull out one of those clips for the cord and a pair of funny-looking scissors.

My focus goes back to Jax sitting at the end of the bed, then it clicks — he's holding our baby in his arms.

"Mr. Travelli, would you like to cut the cord now?" one of the medics asks.

Jax nods his head, looks up at me, and smiles.

"We have a baby girl, Laini. We have a gorgeous baby girl."

I nod and smile. Jax cuts the cord, and the medics take over. They check the baby over to ensure everything is what it should be and pass me the baby wrapped in one of the baby blankets.

My first hold. My smile does not leave my face as I

stare down at my new baby. Jax comes and sits beside us and kisses my lips, then the baby's head.

I glance up at Emma and see she is busy taking photos.

"Emma, come here and meet your baby sister. Take a selfie of the four of us."

She smiles, sits beside me, kisses her baby sister on the head, and then kisses me on the cheek. Then, she lifts the cell phone and begins taking photos.

"Momma, what is her name?"

I look at Jax and smile, then back to Emma. "Her name is Elizabeth. She is named after a good friend of mine. She was known as Betsy, which means daughter."

I glance back at Jax. He smiles and nods. "I love it. A beautiful name."

"Emma, reach for my cell. I want to speak with my sister and Missy."

Emma turns and lifts my cell and passes it to me.

I see my sister and Missy, and I smile. "Hey, guys. I would like you to meet Elizabeth."

Essy and Missy smile and say, "Congratulations, Laini and Jax. Welcome, Elizabeth."

Essy lifts her baby a little higher and says, "I would like to introduce you to our baby girl, Larisa."

Ow wow. My new baby niece. My heart melts. She looks so much like Bella did as a newborn.

"Hello, little Larisa. Welcome to the family."

I then glance at Missy. She smiles and says, "Congratulations. Essy and Dekk. Hello, Larisa." She glances down at her baby, smiles, and then looks at the camera. "I would like to introduce you to Alyana."

Awww. "Hello, Alyana. Congratulations, Missy and Tanner."

One of the medics grabs my attention.

"Excuse me. It is time we moved you both to the ambulance."

I nod. "Thank you. I'll say goodbye to my sister and friend. They, too, have just given birth."

"Really? That is fantastic."

*I*t's amazing how money speaks. Essy and I share the same room with our daughters in the maternity hospital. We've been here for ten hours, and visiting hours are about to begin. We sent word to our friends and extended family to stay away for at least six weeks, especially if they have not had their updated booster shots in their immunization.

Essy and I organize a beautiful bouquet for Missy and a baby gift basket to be sent to the hospital, she is currently in. Missy was meant to give birth in the hospital with us, but instead, she is in her part of New York in another hospital.

Jax and Dekk have gone home a few hours ago to catch up on sleep, then bring the children in to meet their baby sibling. Essy and I managed an hour or so of sleep. But, our little ones do not understand the meaning of lack of sleep and prefer to be fed and changed.

At least we tagged teamed and showered while the other watched our sleeping baby. It is good to be in our clothes again. Flowers have slowly been arriving. Essy even received a bunch of flowers from her mother-in-law. Dekk's other relatives have been sending gifts and flowers throughout the day. My editor and agent have sent cards, flowers, and baby gift baskets. Francine and Neil even sent us flowers and a gift basket.

Essy and I have been taking photos of all the flowers, gifts, and cards to keep a record and thank everyone.

When the boys arrive with the kids, they can take home the baby gift baskets. Essy and I have already agreed to give a couple of our bouquets of flowers to the nurses' station as a thank-you. The smaller bouquets will go to some of the elderly patients who do not have visitors. Basically, the leftover bouquets will be handed out to other new mothers and women patients to brighten their day.

Chapter Sixty-Seven

LAINI

izzy and I have been home for two weeks. This afternoon we are holding a small gathering to welcome Lizzy, Larisa, and Alyana into our family. Tarret is dropping by. This will be his first time seeing the girls in person, as he has been busy on assignment and didn't want to disappoint his new boss — our sister — Essy.

When I think back to when I first met Jax, a lot has changed since we were seventeen. We have come a long way in our lives, and now we have three healthy children.

My sessions with Jeremy have been a lifesaver. Who knew not having any therapy through the years would affect me so much? With all the trauma, my brain got to the point it had enough. I am grateful to Jax and my daughter for being patient and understanding. I don't know what I would do without them in my life.

"Hey, babe. Has Lizzy crashed yet?" I glance at Jax

and then down to Lizzy, who is busy feeding. A grin forms. I am so blessed.

Then it occurs to me Christmas is just around the corner, and I haven't started on any Christmas preparations. I wouldn't mind traveling to Hamilton Island just to get away — get away from the cold — get away and spend time in the sun. I wonder what Jax would think of that?

"What are you thinking about?"

My eyes meet his, and I smile. "I was thinking about heading to Hamilton Island to escape the cold here for Christmas."

Jax nods and sits beside me, wrapping his arm around my shoulders.

"Sounds good. But I heard they had rain there today."

"It's Summer rain, not Winter rain," I say.

Jax quietly laughs. I watch his smile turn into a serious face. "Laini, would you like to spend some time back at Hamilton Island?"

I don't even think about it. I just nod and say, "Yes."

His smile is back, and he leans forward and kisses me again.

"Well, that is good to know because we fly out tomorrow afternoon."

Huh. It takes a few seconds for my brain to register what Jax said. Hamilton Island. Flying. Then it clicks. We're going to Hamilton Island.

My eyes grow wide, and a smile fills my face. If it weren't for the baby in my arms, I would be bouncing around where I sit. "Are you serious right now?"

"As much as one can." He brushes his lips against mine. "First, the girls and their mothers will need to check in with the doctor first. Then, if you all get the go-ahead, we fly out."

I smile again. "When were you going to fill me in?"

He smiles his cheeky grin that I love so much. "When everyone arrived."

"Have I told you lately that I love you?"

He nods. "Maybe this morning," Jax says, then smiles. From the look on his face, I can see he is keeping something back…another surprise, maybe?

I lift my brow in question. "What?"

Jax shakes his head with a smile. See, I knew there was something else.

His face turns serious for a whole of 1.8 seconds before a smile splits across his face. "The boys and I asked your brother and also your dad if they would like to tag along. Some fun in the sun. What do you think?"

I think it is a fantastic idea. "I love it. A Summer Christmas with my family. All the people we love. I can't wait."

Jax stands and lifts a sleeping Lizzy from my arms. "I'll place her in her bed. I've arranged a bubble bath for you. You can soak and relax before everyone arrives."

I shake my head and wonder how I ended up with my thoughtful husband.

The love of my life.

The man I love to the galaxy and back.

My soul mate and the other half of my heart.

My forever love.

♥ Jax. ♥

I hope you enjoyed reading Ghost of a Chance in Love.
Wanting to know what happens to Essy and Missy, they
have their own books.
Insta Bride, The Bodyguard's Convenient Marriage,
Ghost of a Chance in Love, and Secret Heiress.
Available at all good online bookstores.

THANK YOU

Thank you for reading Ghost of a Chance in Love my third contemporary novella containing urban fantasy themes. I hope you enjoyed it, as much as I loved writing about Laini and Jax.

After reading, consider leaving and writing a positive review, even if it is, a few words, 'I loved this book' or 'I enjoyed it! Kept me turning the page.'

It will assist other readers in their choice when selecting their next book to read. By reading this book, you help keep me in work, so pass the word and tell your friends to grab a copy.

If you would like to learn more about what I am writing or competitions, sign up for my newsletter. https://mltompsett.com/newsletter-signup/

Thinking of reading one of my other books, check me out on my website, bookbub, Goodreads, to name a few places.

www.mltompsett.com

ACKNOWLEDGEMENTS

To my special people who I hound and annoy with my writings — you know who you are, thank you from the bottom of my heart. Your advice, ideas, and comments have been invaluable, big hugs guys. Without you, my book would not be finished.

Ange once again, thank you for putting up with me.

As always, thank you, to my boys — big hugs. Your patience for your mother is a miracle. All the times I bug you on our room chat with cover designs. You must have known all those years ago when I taught you how to use a computer, there would come a time when you had to return the favor.

Love you guys 🤍

THANK YOU
AND
HAPPY
READING

Ghost of a Chance in Love

* 9 7 8 0 6 4 5 4 2 4 7 1 3 *